The Billionaire Duke

A Jet City Billionaire Romance

Gina Robinson

THREE JAYS PRESS, LLC
SEATTLE, WASHINGTON

Copyright © 2016 by Gina Robinson.

All rights reserved. No part of this publication may be reproduced, distributed or transmitted in any form or by any means, including photocopying, recording, or other electronic or mechanical methods, without the prior written permission of the publisher, except in the case of brief quotations embodied in critical reviews and certain other noncommercial uses permitted by copyright law.

www.ginarobinson.com

Publisher's Note: This is a work of fiction. Names, characters, places, and incidents are a product of the author's imagination. Locales and public names are sometimes used for atmospheric purposes. Any resemblance to actual people, living or dead, or to businesses, companies, events, institutions, or locales is completely coincidental.

Book Layout ©2013 BookDesignTemplates.com
Cover Design by Jeff Robinson

The Billionaire Duke, The Billionaire Duke Series/Gina Robinson.
— 1st ed.
ISBN 978-0692631874

Also by
GINA ROBINSON
THE BILLIONAIRE DUKE SERIES
Part 1, THE BILLIONAIRE DUKE
Part 2, THE DUCHESS CONTEST

SWITCHED AT MARRIAGE ROMANCE SERIAL
Part 1, A WEDDING TO REMEMBER
Part 2, THE VIRGIN BILLIONAIRE
Part 3, TO HAVE AND TO HOLD
Part 4, FROM THIS DAY FORWARD
Part 5, FOR RICHER, FOR RICHEST
Part 6, IN SICKNESS AND IN WEALTH
Part 7, TO LOVE AND TO CHERISH

NEW ADULT ROMANCE
RUSHED
CRUSHED
HUSHED
RECKLESS LONGING
RECKLESS SECRETS
RECKLESS TOGETHER

SPY CAMP BOOKS
SPY CANDY
SPY GAMES

THE AGENT EX SERIES
"Full of laughter, intrigue, and, of course, steamy spies." —*RT Book Reviews*

THE SPY WHO LEFT ME
DIAMONDS ARE TRULY FOREVER
LIVE AND LET LOVE
LICENSE TO LOVE
LOVE ANOTHER DAY

CHAPTER ONE

Seattle, Washington
Riggins Feldhem

Beauty. Fashion. *Stylish women who knew how to wear clothes.* I loved them in every size and shape. I know. I sounded like a damn designer fashion commercial—*fashion is my passion.* But I founded Flashionista so *every* woman could look and feel her most beautiful. On a budget. While fashion and fulfilling dreams was satisfying, business was *my* passion.

How did I become so successful? Through hard work and determination. And a little bit of luck. Where did I come up with my business ideas, like Flashionista? *Easy.* From needs I saw in real life. Wasn't that where all good ideas came from?

Flashionista was my way of paying homage to my mom. A nod to the woman who'd sacrificed so much to make sure I had a decent life that she'd never had a dime to spare for herself. She'd been beautiful. Everyone who'd known her would tell you that. But after my father abandoned us, something inside her had withered. She never had time to think about herself or money for stylish things to make her feel beautiful again. If Flashionista had been around for her maybe things would have been different.

Necessity was not only the mother of invention, but of innovative new business models. I saw a hole in the market and stepped in to fill it with online fashion flash sales. Thanks to Mom's lack of money, I now had plenty. If she were still alive, she'd be proud of me.

Mom had taught me something else—beauty comes in *all* shapes and sizes. Stylish, sexy clothes weren't just for the tall and gaunt. The pregnant mother-to-be with her beautiful, taut baby bump wanted to feel gorgeous, too. And the curvy woman who wasn't afraid to show off her assets. The new mom just getting her figure back. The tall, boy-figured girl who could wear full pleats or a peplum.

Give me a confident woman. A woman who knew she looked good in her skin was the ultimate turn-on.

It was my mission to make fashionable clothes, jewelry, and accessories affordable to every woman, man, and child. Beautifying America one flash sale at a time. That was me. If that sounded arrogant, I'm sorry. I laugh at myself and my "lofty" ideals all the time. I was just passionate about what I did.

I'd founded Flashionista with programming prodigy Justin Green. Together we'd built a thriving business.

Never one to miss an opportunity to plug my company, I had said all of this in my interview with Seattle's most popular magazine for their annual "most beautiful people" issue. Laying it on thick to make my point. Dressed properly, anyone could be attractive.

No one at the magazine had come right out and said it, but being interviewed implied I was in the running again for Seattle's hottest bachelor. I'd seized the opportunity to promote Flash, as we affectionately called the company.

As I sat in my office and stared at the cover of the advance copy that had been delivered a few minutes earlier by bicycle courier, I shook my head. Lazer Grayson's ugly mug stared back at me as he leaned against one of his vast collection of exotic cars.

I rolled my eyes. Lazer was such a damn showoff.

Lazer was both friend *and* nemesis. We had a friendly, ongoing, unspoken competition over just about everything. He only *thought* he was suave. He could bullshit his way into convincing others of his brilliance. That was his real genius.

We both belonged to the local billionaire's club, the Entrepreneurs, Inventors, and Engineers International Organization, EIEIO, which was a joke of an acronym on purpose. Yeah, like we were all just local farmers growing money on trees.

Lazer was also a mentor to my young business partner Justin. If Lazer ever got the chance, I was certain he would do his damnedest to entice Justin into one of his ventures. He was always poaching.

I didn't understand Justin's friendship with Lazer. Lazer had tried to steal Justin's new wife last year. On the heels of their wedding night. As I said, always poaching. I didn't have a wife. But if I did, I sure as hell wouldn't let another guy get away with hitting on her.

Justin's marriage had been strange. Sudden and unexpected. People had been skeptical it would last. But damn, trying to steal the bride while the honeymoon bed was still warm?

I'd made my views on Lazer known. The rest was Justin's business. That tech-geek-gamer acing me out of the top spot as Seattle's hottest bachelor was both amusing and irritating. Lazer would never let me hear the end of it.

With a sense of morbid curiosity—what the hell did it matter, anyway?—I flipped open the magazine.

Number two. I was damned *number two*. Much smaller picture. Much smaller spread. Much less press for Flash than Lazer's company got. It was better than a swift kick in the butt, but not by much.

Lazer's net worth had inched above mine with the latest acquisition he'd made. As I skimmed the article, it became apparent that little bit of cash had thrown the competition in his favor. That was the only thing he had over me. That and the way he'd flirted with the female interviewer. Which was also obvious from the fawning coverage. Crap, they'd sent a *guy* to interview me.

I grabbed my phone and texted my favorite florist with instructions to send Lazer a nice, girly bouquet of flowers. A spray of fifty pink roses wrapped in paper and tied with a white satin ribbon should do it. I dictated a note. *Congratulations on your pageant win.*

No one could say I was a sore loser.

I was gunning for Lazer. *Next year.*

I didn't plan to marry any time soon. I liked women. Loved them. I just wasn't high on the institution of marriage. Look what it had done for Mom.

Anyway, I hadn't found a woman I was willing to commit to, risk my heart for, and share my billions with. Most of the time I was too damn busy running Flash to have time for anything else.

Justin accused me of being cynical. Maybe I was. I certainly didn't deny it. My experiences with love had led to heartbreak, not happiness.

Maybe I hadn't ever found *real* love, whatever the hell that was. It didn't matter. There wasn't anything lacking in my life. Flash was my passion, my mistress, my love. She was a demanding little obsession at that.

Jennifer, my highly efficient office assistant, poked her head in the door. "Entertaining reading?"

I scowled for comic effect and held the magazine up. "Have you seen this piece of shit?"

"Would you like me to call the editor and complain?" The edges of her lips twitched.

"You're enjoying this too much." I slapped the magazine onto the desk and grinned to show her I was a good sport.

"Not at all, boss. *You* are the hottest bachelor in *my* book. Definitely the hottest boss." She laughed. "Especially when it comes to raise time. Just remember that!"

I rolled my eyes and laughed. "I'm not that obviously vain, am I?"

If I could find a single woman as organized, loyal, good-humored, and tolerant as Jennifer, I might be tempted to marry. But like all the good ones, Jennifer was taken.

"Put your fake scowl away." She stepped in, closed the door, and lowered her voice confidentially. "There's a British gentleman here to see you. And by gentleman, I mean *gentleman*.

"Says he's a solicitor and he has an important family matter to discuss with you." She stepped forward and handed me his card.

Colin Thorne, Senior Partner
Baily, Cragwell, and Thorne Solicitors
London

Shit. What had my black sheep British cousins done now? One of them probably wanted bail money for either herself or her latest loser boyfriend or husband. Or was trying to scam some out of me one way or another.

My dad's side of the family had always been an embarrassment. Including the old man himself. He ran off and abandoned Mom and me when I was just a baby. I'd been the man of the house since I was six months old.

Since I'd founded my first company, the online fashion accessory company before Flash, and made my first several hundred million, Feldhem family members had been coming out of the woodwork with their hands out. Generally obscure and distant British female cousins. As far as I knew, I had no male cousins. At least none had appeared. Cousins I wasn't convinced were really cousins and not fakes and con artists. Like those Nigerian princes.

"Would you like me to tell him you're tied up?" Jennifer said.

I raised an eyebrow at her phrasing. Since *Fifty Shades*, being tied up had a totally different meaning for Seattle billionaires.

Jennifer laughed. "I can send him away."

"How persistent is he?" I asked, trying to gauge what he was up to and what his intent was.

"He impresses me as determined to see you. He may be put off, but he won't be permanently deterred. I could buy you some time to check him out before you meet with him." She paused. "He seems...genuine. Quality. Like I said, a gentleman. Very upper-crust and stiff-upper-lip British."

I valued Jennifer's opinion. She was a good judge of character. She was telling me, in her subtle way, that I should hear this guy out. Which piqued my interest.

I sighed and shook my head. "I have a hole in my schedule right now. Better to get this over with. Send him in."

She put on her professional smile and nodded.

I didn't often take meetings with strangers. Every guy and his dog wanted to see me. Most with a story about why I should part with some of my billions.

I was intrigued and curious. Someone, presumably a family member, had gone to the trouble and expense to send a "quality" British lawyer across the pond to meet with me. That didn't happen every day.

I stood when Mr. Thorne entered the room and extended my hand for a shake as I sized him up. "Riggins Feldhem."

Thorne was exactly as Jennifer described him. Impeccably dressed and groomed. Carrying an expensive briefcase. Not hip, but certainly classic. Middle-aged. Gray at the temples. Tall and thin. A commanding presence. Regal. Gentlemanly.

He didn't look like some fly-by-night shyster with a law degree by mail. If appearances could be believed, he was the kind of lawyer you'd pay a hefty hourly fee to. Though I'd heard British solicitors were underpaid compared to their American counterparts.

"Colin Thorne." He shook my hand heartily, with deference that I appreciated.

"Please. Have a seat." I gestured toward a dark leather armchair at the end of the sofa table, taking the opposite one myself. "If you're here on behalf of one of my distant family members, I can spare you the trouble. I'm not bailing another one out of whatever jam they've gotten into again." I laughed, but I was serious.

"I *am* here about a distant member of your family, actually. But it's more of what they have done for you...sir." His accent was upper crust. That kind of accent that made American women weak in the knees.

There were times when I wished I'd inherited a touch of a British accent. Too bad Dad hadn't stuck around until I could speak.

It may have been my imagination, but Thorne hesitated a fraction of a second before calling me "sir." Almost tripped on it. Like it wasn't *quite* the right way to address me. *Odd.*

"How's that?" I sat and leaned back in my chair, studying him. "Most people come to *me* for favors. Pardon my skepticism, but my family has never done shit for me. They usually want money. Especially my cousin Maggie."

Mr. Thorne's expression was sympathetic. To be honest, he didn't look like the class of lawyer Maggie could afford. Not unless she'd gotten involved in a high-profile class action suit and someone else was paying the tab.

"Let me reassure you, I'm not here to ask you for money. I represent the estate of a late relative of yours. I'm charged with fulfilling the terms of his will and honoring his last wishes." He took a deep breath. "Your father was Basil Julian Feldhem, Junior?"

I nodded, intrigued again by mention of a late relative.

"And he's deceased, is that correct?"

I shrugged. "Is he?" I paused. "You know more than I do. I haven't heard from him since I was a baby. It wouldn't surprise me."

I couldn't decide whether I was relieved by the news or not. If Mom had still been alive, I *would* have been relieved. *Definitely.* In the back of my mind I'd always worried she would take him back if he ever showed up on our doorstep again. And he would break her heart irrevocably. But hadn't he done that already?

"I regret to say he was declared dead some years ago, yes." Thorne, again, looked sympathetic.

"Declared dead?" I studied Thorne closely, on alert. "That's an odd way to put it."

"He was in a boating accident. Went overboard and never resurfaced. His body was never recovered."

"Huh."

Thorne looked surprised by my reaction. "You aren't curious?"

I held his gaze. "Should I be? He was a stranger to me. No more a dad than an anonymous sperm donor from a sperm bank. Any curiosity I had about him was satisfied by my mom. I know what he looked like, what kind of character he had, and what she felt for him. So, no, I'm not. If that makes me seem cold, I'm sorry."

"Not at all." Thorne cleared his throat. "Your father was British. Your mum, American. At one point, you had dual British and American citizenship. Are you still a British citizen?"

It was an odd question. I had no knowledge of British law. Did I have to be a British citizen to inherit whatever the hell it was this late relative had left me? Assuming he, or she, had left me something besides instructions on how to spread the ashes.

"I am, yes. I've maintained my dual citizenship. Mostly because of my mom's wishes. It made her happy, so what the hell? She felt that it could someday be beneficial to me. At the very least, it gives me mystique and appeals to the ladies." I laughed.

Thorne didn't.

"Mom never elaborated. I think she had a thing for British men until the end. She was a complicated and mysterious woman."

Mr. Thorne smiled very slightly and looked almost relieved. Probably not by the idea of my mother being mysterious.

"Brilliant." He paused, put on a serious, lawyerly face, and pulled out an envelope with an official-looking seal. "As His Grace's official emissary and solicitor, I regret to inform you that your cousin, the fourth Duke of Witham, Rans Basil Feldhem the Fourth, passed away Sunday last. Peacefully. In his bed. As was his wish."

Basil must have been a family name for the greater family-at-large.

"I had a cousin who was a duke?" I raised an eyebrow, expecting Thorne to crack and admit he was pranking me.

This was one of the elaborate jokes the EIEIO guys would think up. We were always pranking each other. Because of his latest win as hottest bachelor, Lazer should have been their target. Maybe I should have been flattered that they were expecting me to take the title. In any case, I'd be damned if *I* was going to fall for this and be the butt of their jokes for the next decade.

Thorne was watching me closely. If he expected me to dissolve into tears of grief and renting of my designer suit, he was going to be disappointed.

And so we sat, staring at each other to see who would blink first. A duke? Wait. Weren't all of the princes dukes? Wasn't a duke, a duke who wasn't also a prince, just a step down from royalty? The top rank of the British aristocracy?

Mom hadn't drilled much Britishness or British history into me. But she *had* taught me the old memory trick to remember the aristocratic ranks—do men ever visit Boston? Dukes, marquises, earls, viscounts, barons. Though what Boston had to do with it, I couldn't say. It seemed like an American joke. But then, "great big ducks fear antelopes" neither made sense nor had much to do with music, either. And yet it described the scales of the bass clef and my music teacher, and later my vocal coach, had drilled it into me.

I'd never heard any family lore about being currently related to anyone above the rank of homeless drunk. My family more closely resembled the characters of *Oliver Twist* than anything else. If Thorne had told me I had descended from the inspiration for the Artful Dodger, I wouldn't have been surprised.

I wasn't into genealogy. Hadn't bothered to care about Dad's side of the family. Certainly had no interest in digging it up. Mostly I'd fought to forget it.

Neither Thorne nor I blinked.

Being related to a duke sounded like something out of a fairytale. Or *Now You See Me*. A great, big, fat con.

"A duke? Really?" I said with a high degree of skepticism. "There are, what? About thirty-five non-royal dukes in all of Britain? He was a *British* duke, I assume, given my ancestry. Not Scottish or Irish." I wanted to see how far Thorne would take things.

"Very British," Thorne said. "There are twenty-four non-royal dukes." His expression was neutral as he corrected me.

"Even a rarer breed than I thought." Mine had been an educated guess. I'd overestimated on purpose. It would have been easy enough to Google.

"Your heritage is quite exceptional. The Duke of Witham was created by Queen Victoria in 1874 for the Earl of Witham for his exemplary service to the Crown in India. Highly unusual, given it was rumored he was a spy for the Crown."

"Let me get this straight," I said. "She elevated him from an earl to a duke as a way of saying thank you?"

Thorne nodded. "Precisely."

"For being a spy. Seems like a nice gesture."

"It was brilliant. Very generous of the queen. Spies are rarely given a peerage. And in cases where they inherit a title, prohibited from spying, no matter how honorable the cause. No one trusts a liar, especially with a seat in the House of Lords."

I resisted saying most politicians were liars anyway. A spy was at least honest about it.

"The early earl was, by all historical accounts, a different breed altogether. He was already a spy, and, having been raised in India and serving as a soldier, a bit of a wild hare, when he assumed the earldom.

"He had been far down in the line of succession until a tragic accident took the lives of all direct heirs shortly before his predecessor's death, stunning society. He had neither been raised in society, nor trained in the responsibilities incumbent in the position.

"When the old earl passed on, the first Rans Feldhem, whom the late duke was named after, was a only a distant cousin, but the heir nonetheless." Thorne gave me a piercing look.

History repeating itself, I thought.

"He took on the title to the dismay of many of the peers of his day. It was also rumored that his mother was an Indian rani. Another circumstance not in his favor.

"His countess, however, was lovely. And rumored to have been instrumental in preserving the earldom, and later, growing the holdings of the dukedom. A good duchess can make all the difference to a dukedom."

Thorne crossed his legs and continued his study of me. I assumed I was supposed to be impressed. Or scandalized. He was a good storyteller, if nothing else.

"*If* there *was* a duke in the family, he must have been an embarrassment to the aristocracy," I said, coolly, hoping to make Thorne sweat with my skepticism. And show him I wasn't a sucker easily buying this. Dukes, *right.* "The Feldhems, in my experience, are all reprobates."

"His Grace was an *excellent* lord of the estate." Thorne sounded defensive for the first time. But he made no attempt to reassure me the Dead Duke had been a great guy, well loved, and admired.

There you had it. Power and status didn't make the Dead Duke likable.

"The duke did exist, I assure you," Thorne said, understandably ruffled.

I'd just called him a liar. Politely, but still.

"I have served as his solicitor for many years. But if you would rather not take my word, I have the paperwork with me to prove it." He tapped the envelope. "And you are...incorrect. The name of Feldhem is held in high regard in the highest circles of British society. Every family has its black sheep. It is unfortunate if your association has been with only those members of your family who have not lived up to the name. Rest assured, you can be proud of your ancestry, really."

I shook my head again. I was beginning to believe Thorne. If he was a fake, he was a convincing one. My gut said he was genuine. I hadn't succeeded in business without having a knack for spotting liars. "I would have liked to have met him."

"The late duke was a reclusive man," Thorne said. "And very old. A hundred and five at his passing. He rarely saw visitors. Especially these last twenty-five years. He hadn't allowed children in his presence since 1970, I believe. He didn't like them. I regret to say, he would not have received you."

"Sounds like a great guy." I grinned. "Like the rest of the family." I paused. "You said you have good news? Did he leave me something? A family heirloom?"

"You might say so, yes. He left you a dukedom, Your Grace."

CHAPTER TWO

*R*iggins "Your Grace?" I laughed, not sure I should have been amused. "I'm a duke now, am I?" I shook my head, stunned. If this was true, the selection committee for Seattle's Hottest Bachelor was going to be sorry they hadn't waited a few days to make their decision. A duke, real aristocracy, a real title, had to beat Lazer out of hottest bachelor status.

"You'll forgive my disbelief," I said. "Now I *will* have to see some proof."

Thorne shoved the envelope across the coffee table to me. "It's all in there."

I took the envelope, opened it with a cautious eye on Thorne, and skimmed the paperwork. It looked legit to me. I would, of course, run it past my lawyer, Harry

Lawrence. Still wary, I quickly Googled the Duke of Witham. Dozens of news articles in British newspapers and blogs about him, and his recent death, popped up. It would have been hard to fake this much coverage.

I shoved the paperwork back across the table to Thorne and made a snap decision. I didn't need this shit. The headaches of running a dukedom, however small, on top of Flash? A dukedom was like a small company in itself. My life was good as it was.

"I decline. Sorry for your trouble." I rocked forward in my chair, ready to stand and see him to the door.

Thorne remained seated, clearly not taking the hint. "I'm sorry, Your Grace. You can't decline. It's a hereditary title. It's yours whether you want it or not. What you do with it is, of course, your business. Within the bounds of the entailment."

He paused. "Now that I've delivered the news, shall I schedule a meeting through your assistant to go over the details of the estate and your new responsibilities?"

I paused, choosing my words carefully. "I'm honored. I am. I'm sure there are plenty of British men who would kill to be dukes. There has to be someone else who can take the title and do a damn fine job with it.

"But I'm an American, more than anything. I don't have the vaguest idea *how* to be a duke. I understand only enough to realize that if there's an estate involved, I simply don't have time to run it. Or be as involved as a duke should be." I stood. "There aren't enough hours in the day as it is. With all due respect, I abdicate, then."

"You can't abdicate. Only kings and queens abdicate. The only way to lose the title is through death." There was that sympathetic look again. "About that meeting?"

I dropped back into my chair and glanced at my watch. Thorne had been in my office less than ten minutes and had managed to turn my life entirely upside down. What the hell kind of havoc could he wreak in an hour or more?

I drummed my fingers on my desk, irritated with this new nuisance, trying desperately to come up with a way to get out of it. "I have a few minutes still. Now is as good a time as any."

I grabbed my phone and texted Jennifer to make sure I wasn't disturbed, and asked her to reschedule my afternoon meetings. I got the feeling this might take a while. And afterward, I'd need a stiff drink. "Let me just call my lawyer. Harry can be here in a few minutes."

"Of course, you will want your solicitor to look over the paperwork. But may I request a few minutes first, to go over the essential details in private?"

I stared at Thorne, not liking the direction this was taking. I shrugged. "All right. Give it to me straight. Was the family's ancestral home lost to taxes years ago?"

I was hoping to get lucky and be a duke mostly in title only. Hoping there was very little left to the estate.

Contrary to Thorne's assertion, if the Dead Duke had been a *true* Feldhem, he would have mismanaged everything he touched and squandered every penny he'd inherited.

"Actually, Your Grace, I'm happy to report that your finances are remarkably sound. Witham House is a beautiful estate on three thousand acres, fully and gorgeously maintained and restored by the late duke. You have inherited no debt at all. Even after inheritance taxes, you will still be a wealthy man."

I shook my head and laughed. "Of course I will! I'm a billionaire in my own right."

"My mistake. I should have said the dukedom alone would make you a wealthy man. In your particular case, your wealth will increase."

"Good," I said, taking a fair amount of joy out of being wealthier than Lazer. There *was* that.

Thorne pulled more paperwork out of his briefcase. "All of the details of your inheritance are contained here, in the late duke's will. Along with instructions on your responsibilities as the new duke."

I took them without looking at them. "I don't need to see these. I'll hand them off to my lawyer and see what he makes of them. As for being the new duke"—I grinned—"that's easy. If I have to keep the title, fine. I'll be a duke in title only. I'm not leaving Seattle and my business for England. I'm liquidating the estate at the first opportunity."

Thorne watched me impassively, almost as if he'd been expecting my reaction. "The estate is *entailed*, Your Grace."

Obviously, I wasn't ignorant of business affairs, but I was unschooled in British inheritance laws.

"Meaning?" I said.

"You don't own the title to the property outright. You are restricted from selling it by the terms of the entailment, which were set up centuries ago." He paused, studying me with a masked expression. "You obviously understand corporations. Think of the entailment like a corporation. It is a legal body that continues to exist over generations. Ideally, it holds wealth indefinitely and passes the power of wealth down the family line. In this case, to you. You are only the trustee, the steward, the CEO of this corporation for your lifetime."

"Are you sure I can't pass this title and estate onto the next in line?" I was grasping for anything.

"*You* are the last in line, the last living Feldhem male. There *is* no one else."

I cursed beneath my breath. "So I'm stuck with this?"

I was still trying to come to terms with my new "good fortune." Just my luck to be stuck with an albatross. I thought suddenly of Mom and her insistence that I maintain my British citizenship. Had she known this was a possibility?

"I have no ties, no sentimental attachment either to my family or to the family estate. I haven't been raised or trained to be a duke. I'm incredibly busy running my own business. I don't have time to run a dukedom. It won't be my top priority.

"Three thousand acres?" I whistled beneath my breath. "And an estate. I'm just not a good candidate for the job. What happens if I mismanage the estate?

Or lose it? The best I can do is hire a competent manager. And you know how being an absentee owner goes. No one cares as much as the owner." I laughed softly at the irony. "Generally, anyway." I sighed. "Competent managers are hard to find..."

I paused, my mind racing to find a solution. "Here's an idea—what if I donate it to the National Trust? Is there anything in the law that forbids me from donating it for the enjoyment of the British people? That way everyone wins."

Thorne sighed. "The late duke anticipated your reaction. It was his express desire to keep the estate privately held by the family. He spent his life working toward that goal.

"In light of that, he put restrictions in place to keep an irresponsible heir from destroying the dukedom and the family legacy. Or from disposing of the estate in any way. Most importantly, the late duke has made what I believe you American businessmen call a poison pill?"

I stared at Thorne. "What do you mean? What are you talking about?" Just how diabolical and smart was the Dead Duke? Maybe he was a true Feldhem, after all.

"As I said, you are the last of a long line of Feldhems. The last male heir. If you die, or destroy the dukedom, the line dies out and the title goes extinct.

"The Crown has stated that it will make no new dukedoms. Non-royal dukes are a dying breed. And despite the rules of succession changing for the Crown to allow a female heir to the throne, nearly all dukedoms, including yours, still operate under the male-heir-only rules of earlier centuries. It's almost impossible for a female to become duchess by inheriting. Duchesses are only created by marriage.

"The late duke, knowing you were raised as an American with little regard for our traditions and history, and no knowledge, let alone love, for Witham House and your family dynasty, made certain provisions that make not succeeding as the Duke of Witham and properly maintaining the dukedom highly undesirable to you, I should imagine."

I laughed. "What could the Dead Duke possibly do to me?"

Hubris always goes before a fall.

"The late duke, while reclusive, was astute. And a studious observer of human nature. He knew how to find a man's vulnerabilities and exploit them. He was sharp and in possession of his full mental faculties to the end.

"I think, if I were to speculate, that plotting how to keep his current heir in line after his death contributed to his longevity and clarity of mind."

"Wonderful," I said. Was I supposed to be impressed? Had Thorne just handed me the secret to long life? "He couldn't just do the daily crossword or a sudoku?"

Thorne smiled, very slightly. "The late duke had many faults. None having to do with money. He was an expert investor. As you will find out soon enough, the assets of the dukedom must only be used for your support and the continued support of the dukedom.

"The late duke, however, had a small fortune from his mother's side that was not subject to the entailment. He became a multimillionaire by investing it. But, as you Americans also say, you can't take it with you.

"The most important thing to the late duke was his legacy. He wanted the family name and the dukedom to continue. He realized, too late in life, that he would not produce his own heir. Since your father's death, you have been the heir presumptive, and the duke has been studying you."

"That isn't at all creepy," I said, managing not to shudder.

Thorne actually laughed. "You made it easy on him by keeping a high profile. If it is any consolation, he liked you. He was pleased you would be succeeding him. I believe that made his final days easier and more peaceful. He had great faith that you could keep the estate intact and hand it in good condition to your own son one day."

"Glad I could be of service," I said, not bothering to hide my sarcasm. "He should have been grateful my father died before me. Dad could have ruined the estate with ease. Damn, Dad. He screwed me over in so many ways. Even by dying."

Thorne didn't look amused. He became suddenly serious again. "The late duke believed you and he were very alike. You have the same talent with money and business. A man with your skills should be able to keep the dukedom thriving through your lifetime with relative ease. And pass it along to an equally worthy heir."

Thorne paused. "The late duke assumed, being so much like him, that you would understand about legacies and wouldn't want your dynasty taken from you or your life's work destroyed."

I hadn't been taking Thorne's tone seriously. Now he had my full attention. "Is that a threat?"

"Take it any way you will," Thorne said. "When your company went public last year, the late duke bought fifteen percent of it through his various holding companies.

"If you don't take your duties as the duke seriously, and follow the late duke's last wishes exactly, as executor of his will, I'm under orders to use the power that accompanies owning those shares to ruin Flashionista. I have expert investors to help me. I will dump the shares on the market, if necessary."

I swallowed hard as I took in the implications of what he was saying. "But that will—"

"Cause a panic? A run on the shares? Drive the price to pennies on the dollar? Ruin you? Bankrupt Flashionista?" Thorne nodded. "Yes. True. All true. The duke is deceased. He has nothing to lose but his legacy. The continuation of the dukedom was the most important thing to him. He was willing to allocate all of his resources to insuring that legacy continues."

If this all hadn't been so bizarre, I might not have believed Thorne. I went over the IPO in my mind. "We were so careful—"

"And the late duke exceptionally clever. He was, as I said, an expert investor."

I needed time to check the facts and make sure what Thorne was alleging was actually true. "What does the Dead Duke want from me?"

I was buying time. If what Thorne said was true, there *had* to be a workaround.

"That you do your duty. It's all in that envelope. In short, however, he wants you to do what all good dukes must do—marry and produce a male heir. And a spare would be nice, though not required under the terms the late duke specified. Though I believe there may be a bonus for one."

I snorted. "You've got to be kidding? This is the twenty-first century!"

Thorne sat calmly, legs still crossed. "The late duke had no sense of humor. He didn't joke, I assure you."

"What are the terms?" I said as I frantically tried to find an out. "I assume there's a timeline?"

I sure as hell would have made a timeline. It was time to start thinking like my adversary.

"The late duke specified that you must be married by midnight of the date one month from the date of his death. In this case, Valentine's Day."

Damn.

"Pacific Standard Time, I hope." I tried to keep calm and match Thorne's demeanor while I plotted a way to escape this fate. "I would hate to be caught by a technicality."

"Exactly so, Pacific Standard Time."

"I'm not even seeing anyone. What does the Dead Duke want me to do? Advertise for a bride?" I laughed. The whole situation was ridiculous.

"Surely, Your Grace, getting a bride shouldn't be a difficulty for Seattle's Second Hottest Bachelor?" He had the traces of a tease in his voice.

Did Thorne actually have a sense of humor? Damn that magazine article that was sitting open on my table. Thorne must have been able to read upside down.

"Less than a month isn't even enough time for a bride-to-be to get a decent wedding gown, let alone plan a wedding. Assuming there was already a bride-to-be." I shook my head. "The Dead Duke wants me to snap up just *any* bride?"

I snorted, losing my amusement at the situation. There were adventures. And there were disasters. This was shaping up to be the latter. "He's not as discriminating as I would have expected about the mother of his future heirs!

"Isn't a year more traditional and a more reasonable amount of time to find a wife? If there's ever a timeline stipulated in stories and movies, it's always a year. What's the damn hurry?" I was hoping to buy some time.

"I'm a young man," I argued. "I need more than a damn month to find the right girl and fall in love." Not that that seemed likely. "Even a matchmaking service will need more than that."

Thorne nodded. "I appreciate your concerns. The late duke was a cautious man. Because you are the last male Feldhem, there *is* no time. If something should happen to you..."

He let the unsaid hang in the air a moment. "Being in love has never been a prerequisite for aristocratic British marriages. Lineage, breeding, family name, and money are much more important."

I sighed, heavily, wondering how I could outwit him.

"Once again, you underestimate the late duke," Thorne said. "He was supremely concerned about the mother of his continuing line. Before his death, he, in essence, picked out your bride."

"What the hell!"

Thorne ignored my outburst. "The late duke wants his bloodline to merge with his American first wife's, as he believes it should have in the first place. His will stipulates you must marry a single, childbearing woman from her line." He paused. "There is only one woman left who meets the requirements."

Of course there is. Fantastic. An arranged marriage. What's next?

"So who is this woman?" I said, hoping she would be as against marrying a stranger as I was. And not a complete mess.

Haley Hamilton

I needed a hero. But I wasn't likely to find one inside The Blackberry Bakery. I'd worked here a full year already and none had come charging in. Or even sauntered in. I would take sauntering. Sure.

Our customers leaned toward mostly female. A lot of the trendy crowd of girls who worked at Flashionista just a few blocks away. They were all gorgeous, thin, and dressed to kill any aspirations I had of landing one of the few hetero guys who came through our doors. Or frequented the local happy hour at the bar down the street.

Since the big tech boom in Seattle, we'd had an influx of nerdy, techie guys who earned good money. Supposedly guys now outnumbered available girls in Seattle. Desperate guys eager to impress the girls. For all the good it did me. They were all congregated in a section of Seattle ten blocks east. In my area of town, men were still scarce.

It wasn't my finest hour. I was barefaced. My hair was in a loose bun and net. I was covered in flour. My forearm had a raised, blistered welt from a hot tray of muffins that got a little too close as it came out of the oven. My finger was bandaged—too exuberant with a paring knife while slicing apples for the apple tarts. And I was sweaty and exhausted.

At one point I had loved baking, right? Who had talked me into ditching my business degree and pursuing baking as anything more than a hobby?

Oh, *right*. That would be me. Baking had been so much fun before pastry school. Back in the days I'd baked with lots of love for friends and family. And experimented with my own creativity.

But doing anything for a job sucked the fun out of it. Work was called *work* for a reason. Commercial baking required early hours that went against my constitution, and demanded physical strength. After my first month on the job, I'd canceled my gym membership. I'd lifted so much weight at the bakery that I was in danger of looking like one of those female bodybuilders, all brawn and veiny muscles.

Okay, that was a slight exaggeration. But not much. I could make a muscle that at least a few guys would envy. My usually scrawny thighs had definition and were getting almost too large for my skinny jeans. And yesterday someone had called me "mister."

And now I'd been reduced to wanting a hero for nothing more than the mundane task of all this heavy lifting. I'd been up since two a.m. I was dead on my feet. Where was my knight on a fiery steed riding in to take me away from all this?

The lunch rush was lasting later than usual.

Sally, the owner, hustled into the kitchen. "I hate flu season! Hate it! Another one of the girls called in sick." She glanced around the bakery desperately.

I ducked. I knew what she was after. Poof! She wanted to turn a baker into a waitress. I'd put myself through college waitressing. I hated it. I would rather sling fifty-pound bags of flour and heavy trays of baked goods, even if it meant another pan burn. The office world was looking better and better. I turned my back to Sally a fraction of a second too late.

"Haley!"

"Tag! *You're* it." My fellow baker Cody sniggered and nudged me with his elbow.

Cody was like six feet and two-fifty, a former lineman. He could lift trays all day long.

"Shut your ugly mug," I said, completely devoid of affection.

He laughed outright.

Sally tossed me a waitress apron with the Blackberry logo. "You'll have to do."

Carrying heavy trays of food was no more fun or less physical work than working in the kitchen. Sally didn't know that next to Mary, who was fifty if she was a day, I was probably the most experienced waitress in her employ. I hadn't helped with the impression. Had I intentionally done a mediocre job the few times I'd been called on to fill in?

I wouldn't go that far. But I hadn't exactly tried to excel, either. Do a job badly enough and you won't be called on to do it again. But I didn't want to get fired, either. It was a delicate balance.

I rushed to the bathroom and changed out of my baker's whites.

When Mary saw me coming, she grimaced. "You have flour on your nose." She shook her head. "Wipe it off and work the counter."

I wiped the tip of my nose with the back of my hand. "Better?"

She rolled her eyes. "You could take a little trouble with your appearance."

At two a.m. Was she kidding? To work in the back in the middle of hot ovens? All the bakers did the same thing. Rolled out of bed and into their whites. Put their hair in a net, grabbed a cup of coffee, and ran out the door. What masochist bothered with makeup that would only melt off in the heat?

Working the counter was the grunt work job out front in customer land. You got a lot of work and no tips to augment your meager wage.

The Blackberry Bakery was part bakery and part café. It was open from six a.m. to three p.m. daily. We served sandwiches, soup, coffee, tea, and baked goods made fresh in the back. Customers lined up in front of a long glass bakery case, picked their pastry, ordered their other food, and wound around the L-shaped counter to the register to pay. They took their pastry, found a table, and waited for their order to be delivered. Not the most elegant system, but it worked.

The Blackberry was one of the top bakeries in the city, known particularly for its pastries and breads. It provided baked goods to many of the top Seattle restaurants. But it also made custom cakes for special occasions and weddings. None of the prestige of the bakery made working the counter any more fun or exciting. Hungry people were grumps. And people on limited lunch hours or coffee breaks, even testier.

The line was long and filled with fashionable Flashionistas. Girls who'd taken the time to apply makeup and do their hair for work. I was taking and filling orders from the pastry case so fast, the line became a blur and a cloud of perfume. I no longer saw individual faces.

The bakery was loud with voices, laughter, and the clinking of ceramic plates and flatware.

"Welcome to the Blackberry. What can I get you?" I said to the next person in line without looking up.

"A flat white."

At the sound of the deep, almost melodic male voice, I looked up into the dark brown smiling eyes of Riggins Feldhem and time stood still. Like literally stood still.

It was an earth-shattering moment. One of those you feel only once in a lifetime. Our eyes met. And held. His were searching and intimate and crinkled at the edges as he smiled. He studied me so intently, it took my breath away. My heart raced. The timeline of my life had somehow shifted. I felt it.

It was one of those moments I dreamed about. A chance meeting with a billionaire. A tall, dark, *hot* billionaire who occasionally came into the bakery. Making the dream not all that farfetched. The kind of moment that made me almost automatically reach up to pat my hair like an old lady from the fifties. And here I was without even a touch of clear lip gloss on.

"And one of those delicious chocolate mint brownies." His eyes danced as he studied me.

Riggins always looked like the world amused him. Which intrigued me. Today there was the slightest edge to him, as if he was looking at me with some purpose in mind. With real interest in who I was. Like he was really trying to see me, the *real* me. To say it was flattering was an understatement. Being looked at like that by a man was what women dreamed of.

"If they're any good today," he said, bringing me back to the moment.

I felt ridiculously happy. And nervous. Flustered.

"They're delicious. The best. I made them myself."

Too braggy? I hoped not. I was nervous as I smiled back at him, trying to look flirty without being obvious enough to catch Sally's attention. I was in an apron. How does one look flirty in a work apron?

"Confident," he said. "I like that. You take pride in your work."

"Why not? I was top of my class in pastry school." Bragging again. Why did I keep bragging?

"You've convinced me. One chocolate mint brownie made by"—he glanced at my nametag—"Haley, with confidence."

And love. Or maybe it was only a deep crush on him. I knew he loved chocolate mint brownies. He sent his admin in for them on a regular basis. I always baked them with him in mind.

His grin spread into a full smile. He turned to an older guy next to him. "What will you have, Thorne?"

I hadn't noticed the other guy before.

"The brownies are delicious." Riggins winked at me.

"Tea and one of those biscuits will do." The older guy pointed to a tray of cookies in the case. He had a delightful British accent.

I didn't want to let them go. But I was tongue-tied and the line was growing behind them, buzzing with impatience. I couldn't think of any way to hold them.

Riggins Feldhem had winked at me. I felt way too happy about that.

I got the British guy the best "biscuit" I could find. And served Riggins the perfect brownie right from the center of the pan. And reluctantly passed them off to the cashier.

If my life had been a fairytale, Riggins would have asked me out. But it wasn't. Instead, he paid and took a table by the window. I had to force myself to concentrate on my work and not stare at his table all the time.

I looked up once later to catch my breath and saw Riggins and the older guy still sitting, heads bent close in conversation, glancing at the pastry counter when they thought I wasn't looking.

Riggins was a celebrity. And single. Sally had given us strict instructions to treat him like a normal person. That included keeping the customers from gawking at him as much as possible. And absolutely no flirting with him. Or asking him for pictures. No selfies with him in the background "photo-bombing" the shot. Anyone who violated her rules was subject to immediate firing.

I sometimes wondered if Riggins had paid her off for the protection. She had the same rules for all the Flash execs who came in. But Riggins was the only one who made my pulse race. I usually only caught glimpses of him from the kitchen.

He was a semi-regular on weekdays. I had never gotten to serve him before. More often than not, though, he sent his OA, Jennifer, in to do his bidding and pick up his favorite sandwich and pastry. I knew all his favorites. I took extra care making the chocolate mint brownies and blackberry muffins because I knew those were his favorites.

He was sipping his flat white and staring at me.

Wait? Staring at *me*? I almost looked around to see who was standing next to me. He couldn't be staring at *me*. That had to be my imagination. Riggins Feldhem was consistently on Seattle's Hottest Bachelors list. He might have qualified as a hero in my opinion, if I'd ever thought I had even the faintest prayer of catching his attention. But why would he notice *me*?

Although, he *had* winked at me.

He was totally hot. Always dressed in the latest fashions. And he was probably ten years older than I was. There was nothing about me that would attract a guy like him. Certainly not compared to the sea of gorgeous Flashionista girls around him all day long at the office, and currently at nearby tables here.

Despite all that, he flustered me. I felt myself blush as he studied me. Did I still have flour on my nose? I wiped it again to make sure.

I turned my attention back to the line of customers, still feeling his gaze on me. Every time I looked up, some combination of Riggins and the older guy he was with was watching me. With curiosity. I didn't understand any of it.

Quitting time couldn't come soon enough.

The older guy got a call and got up to take it outside, where it was quieter. The steady line of customers began to slow. I felt almost like I could breathe again as I bent down to get the last brownie out the case for an old couple who wanted two forks so they could share. I turned behind me to grab the forks from the silverware tray.

Sally came out of the kitchen with two plates of food. She looked harried. She thrust the plates into my hands. "Take these to table four."

"That couple needs their forks," I said, nodding behind me.

"I'll get them." She gave me a gentle shove toward the dining area.

Table four was right next to Riggins. It was tight between tables, especially when they were all filled and the customers had moved chairs around. Four chatting Flashionistas had pulled chairs around a two-person table in my path. None of the other routes to table four looked any better.

I went for it, figuring I could shoot the gap. I was halfway through when one of the girls slid back, right into me. Upsetting the delicate balance of the plates. And me.

The plates tipped forward. The soup sloshed. The sandwiches slid forward. I overcorrected, trying to keep from dumping the lunches I was carrying on an unsuspecting Flashionista, or worse, Riggins. And caught the toe of my tennis shoe in the metal scrollwork of the foot of a chair. The soup bowls slid off and hit the floor with a crash of breaking ceramics. Followed by the sandwiches, the plates, and me.

I landed on my knees and palms in the middle of a puddle of chicken soup. Right at that moment, it wasn't curing my ills.

My pants were soaked. My blouse was splattered. My hair was coming out of my bun. I blew my bangs out of my face, blushing to the roots of my colorful hair.

The room went quiet. Someone stifled a laugh. Someone else tittered, giving everyone else permission to laugh at my mishap. I blushed. I just hoped no one had caught my fall on their phone and was in the middle of submitting it to *America's Funniest Home Vide-*

os. From deep in my embarrassment, I heard the scrape of a chair scooting back.

I looked up to see a long-fingered hand reaching down to me. A strong, masculine hand cuffed in a finally tailored dress shirt that peeked beneath a gray suit.

"Take my hand. Let me help you up." Riggins Feldhem smiled down at me.

His smile encouraged me. His grip was firm. His hand was almost scorching as he pulled me to my feet. My heart raced. I was *so* embarrassed. And thrilled at the same time.

He handed me his cloth napkin and looked around for help. "We need a mop over here." He motioned to Mary, who was frowning.

He turned back to me. "It wasn't your fault, Haley. You were accidentally tripped as a chair scooted out."

Up close, he smelled incredible. Who needed a fiery steed when a hero like Riggins had helped me up?

"I can take you away from all this." Riggins Feldhem grinned at me, his dark, sexy eyes snapping.

CHAPTER THREE

*R*iggins
This girl with chicken soup on her knees and no makeup was incredibly cute, even if it was hard at this moment to imagine she was the girl from the impeccable bloodline. The next Duchess of Witham. There was something touching about her fresh-faced innocence and the way she blushed. Something that reminded me of the first girl I'd ever loved, before she became more jaded about love than I was.

I was grateful that the Dead Duke hadn't sent me off to England to woo a British noblewoman, one who knew how a duke was supposed to act. Who wouldn't have given me that hero-worship look simply because I'd offered her a hand up from an embarrassing situation. I was much more comfortable with an American girl.

Pragmatically, it would have been better for at least *one* of us to have had *some* training in how to behave in British society. Been raised by a proper British nanny and sent to an exclusive public school. Someone who traveled in the right circles and knew the right high-society people. Someone who grew up living the life.

I still had trouble believing the mess I was in. It was such a great joke. I almost wished I'd thought it up and sprung it on Lazer. Just to see his face. Was this the Dead Duke's great prank on *his* peers? An American duke with an American duchess who worked in a bakery? Take that and stuff it up yours, peerage.

I was thirty-three. Used to dating experienced women within a few years of my own age. With her wide-eyed expression, the barefaced girl covered in chicken broth and noodles looked about seventeen. My heart squeezed. I was reacting to her. Like a whiff of a pleasant scent from the past, she stirred a memory of a younger, more vulnerable version of me. A guy who'd wanted to believe in happily-ever-afters. *Shit.*

I hardened my heart. I hoped Thorne's information was correct and she wasn't jailbait, because she sure as hell looked it.

Thorne had shared his dossier on her with me during lunch. The good old Dead Duke had been watching her, too. I wondered what the old boy had on her. I'd asked Thorne as much. He'd smiled and said the late duke left nothing to chance. I could rest assured the girl would take me up on my offer to make her my duchess.

"And if she doesn't?" I'd asked, hopefully. "I can't *force* a woman to marry me. There has to be an out for that."

Thorne had maintained his calm, masked expression. "The late duke can force her hand."

"But if he can't?"

"Then, yes, you would have an out, in a manner of speaking." He looked me directly in the eye. "Providing you haven't murdered her or intentionally forced her away."

"No acting like a douche to chase her off. Is that what I'm hearing?" I grinned.

He smiled, very slightly. But extremely slyly.

"And you would be the judge of that, I assume?" I wanted to know how much power Thorne had.

"Yes, Your Grace. Naturally."

Damn.

"Is there any penalty for me if she refuses?" I tried to not to tip my hand.

"The estate is yours, regardless," Thorne said.

"And the extra money, the part that isn't entailed?"

"If she refuses, it's yours on the birth of an heir."

"And the poison pill?"

"Held over your head, I'm afraid, until you sire a son. As long as you're making a good faith attempt, the pill remains in the cupboard, so to speak."

I wanted to see Haley for myself before deciding how to proceed. Although I didn't want to be a duke, I could handle having the title. Specifically, I didn't want the estate and all the headaches associated with it. Nor did I want a wife and the task of "siring an heir" as Thorne so bluntly and Britishly put it during lunch. As if I was a racehorse put out to stud.

There *had* to be a way out of this mess. I just needed a little time. More importantly, in the short term, I needed an ally. Particularly, I needed Haley Hamilton.

A sprig of parsley had somehow lodged on her nametag during her spill. She was small and thin, almost waiflike. Her hand delicate and weightless in mine. With large eyes that were striking for being two different colors—one green, one blue. And lashes so pale she looked almost lash-less. Her hair was bleached blond and pulled severely back. Her bangs were tipped with lavender and pink. Even being so thin, she reminded me of one of the cupcakes topped with pink frosting in the case. Totally tempting.

"You could take me away from all this?" She picked a limp circle of cooked carrot off her blouse. "Are you kidding? Why would I ever want to leave this place?"

I laughed. She had a sense of humor. "We could use a baker who doubles as a waitress who knows how to take a fall in Flash's cafeteria."

"For comedic effect?" She shook her head and smiled up at me from beneath those pale lashes. "Do your waitresses often fall? Sounds like you'll have workmen's comp breathing down your neck soon. Maybe not a good work environment for me." Her smile was radiant.

And still full of that heart-wrenching hero look.

I was hoping to get to know her, my mind racing and plotting a way to ask her out for something innocuous like coffee. Something that wouldn't look like I was moving too fast, or was too eager, and that would satisfy Thorne. And give me a chance to talk with her privately and propose my plan. Once I came up with one.

"Why do you need a baker?" Her eyes danced with tease. "I didn't think you did any baking at the Flashionista cafeteria. Don't you order all your baked goods from commercial bakers? Do you even have any ovens?"

I was about to reply when Sally arrived with a junior employee carrying a mop and bucket, apologizing all over herself.

"I'm so sorry, Riggins. I should know better than to send bakers out to do a waitress's job." She cast a disgusted glance at Haley. "Go on to the back and get cleaned up!"

"No harm done." I flashed Haley my most charming smile.

She smiled back at me and headed toward the counter before I could say more.

Thorne came back inside, pocketing his phone. He caught her attention, said something to her in a low voice I couldn't hear, and handed her his card. Arranging my marriage?

I caught the word "inheritance" and "meet with you" and turned away.

The solicitor had promised me a look at my future bride. I'd argued for a chance to get to know her. There had to be something Harry and my financial guys could do. I needed to talk to Justin, too. Warn him about this new threat. See if he had any solutions.

I waited for Haley to turn and stare at me. To gape. *You mean I have to marry* him? Not to be narcissistic, but I wasn't insecure. I was, after all, the *second* hottest bachelor in the city. If nothing else, my money was an enticement. And now there was the added incentive of my title.

She surprised me by looking surprised, but not at me. She pulled her phone from her pocket and typed something in. To her calendar, I guessed. She shook Thorne's hand and disappeared behind the counter and into the bakery without looking back.

Thorne smiled at me. "Our work here is finished."

"What did you say about me?" I whispered.

"I didn't mention you at all. You're on the agenda for tomorrow's meeting." He gave me that calm, inscrutable look again. "Did you ask her to meet you at a local pub for drinks later for some alcohol-fueled flirting? A little Dutch courage never hurts. You might even work up the nerve to call her a silly cow." He actually winked at me.

"Call her a cow? Do you want her to walk out on me?" I shook my head and gave him a puzzled look. "Who taught *you* how to flirt?"

He looked at me, confused. "It works well in Britain. It's a term of endearment."

"No wonder the line is dying out. You Brits don't know how to flirt.

"And no, asking her for drinks would be moving too fast. We aren't in Italy or France. Seattle girls are aloof. You have to charm them and let them warm up to you. Haven't you ever heard of playing hard to get?" I tossed a tip on the table.

Since Seattle had enacted the fifteen-dollar minimum wage, the tip was included in most bills. I didn't give a shit and left a twenty. Better to be known for being generous. Especially now that I was trying to impress Haley.

I walked out with Thorne and waited on the corner with him for his Uber.

"What do you think of her?" He seemed genuinely interested.

What did I think? There was no reason to hold back my honest opinion. But no reason to spill my guts, either. "She's young."

He smiled. "Not as young as she looks, as you know. And surprisingly tough, resilient, and determined. Excellent qualities for a duchess." He paused. "And did I mention, loyal. Extremely loyal to those she loves."

I had no idea how he knew I prized loyalty above just about everything else. I shrugged. "Nice to know."

"You'll like her better when you get to know her."

I couldn't resist yanking Thorne's chain. "I have no intention of getting to know her better," I said, deadpan. "As soon as we're married, I'm sending her to England. To Witham House. To learn how to be a lady."

"You're going to lock her away like Bluebeard?" Thorne said in his cool, upper crust tone.

I laughed and pointed a trigger-finger at him. He was too much fun to tease. "Got you, Thorne!" I paused. "I'm not a douche. But I thought you'd be pleased. For the late His Grace. Wouldn't it be nice to have the mistress of the manor onsite?

"And think of *her* happiness as well as the Dead Duke's. An adventure in England. Mistress of a historic manor house. What American girl wouldn't jump at the chance?"

Thorne raised an eyebrow.

"If you're going to force me into marriage, I'm going to have the perfect one." I couldn't help myself. I continued the joke. "Perfect harmony. Perfect agreement. Perfectly pleasant to each other.

"The best way to insure a perfectly happy marriage to a complete stranger is to be on separate continents with an ocean between us as much as possible. Perfect happiness is really only a matter of distance and personal space."

Thorne shook his head. "After you get her pregnant, I hope." There was a twinkle in his eyes.

Damn. He was teasing back.

I grinned. "We're living in the twenty-first century, Thorne. We don't need to be on the same continent for *that*. A dirty movie and a cup. A little wrist action. A spin in a centrifuge to separate the Y boys from the Xs and up our odds of a little heir. There's no time to monkey around or take a chance we'll get a girl the first time out. What if I'm hit by a bus? No, this is serious business, Thorne."

I warmed to my joke. "A freezer. A turkey baster. And we're good. No scandal."

"A true romantic, Your Grace." There was a hint of humor in his face. "Ah! There's my car." Thorne waved at it.

"I'm surprised the Dead Duke didn't think of this himself. He could have used a surrogate," I said. "Frozen his sperm and gotten a posthumous heir."

"The heir has to be legitimate," Thorne said, deadpan. "Since the duke would not have married a surrogate—"

"This really is from another century," I said, shaking my head. "You Brits!"

"May I remind you, *you* are a Brit, too." He paused. "The late duke had no desire to marry again. And even if he had, getting a widow pregnant after the duke's demise is a quagmire of legal ambiguity. By then the new heir would have taken the dukedom." He eyed me.

"I wouldn't have contested it." I grinned.

"The late duke believed in tradition, in doing things the traditional way. Without scandal."

"You mean he thought he was living in a Regency novel!"

Thorne gave me a startled look.

"Yes, I know what the Regency period is. Mom used to read a bunch of Regency romances." I paused. "Maybe she knew something."

Thorne's car pulled to the curb. "I'm meeting with Miss Hamilton tomorrow morning at ten. Be at the rented office tomorrow by eleven.

"I'll have the late duchess' engagement ring with me for you to give to Miss Hamilton. It's been in the family for nearly a hundred years. It's beautiful and extremely valuable. I think it will be appropriate."

He gave me a dry look. "Do try to think of something appropriately romantic to say to the young woman when you ask for her hand. The late duke specified that you should make an actual marriage proposal. He wanted this marriage to get off on the best possible footing."

I kept the sarcastic remark dancing on the end of my tongue to myself.

"In the meantime, don't worry about informing the press of your change in circumstances. While we've been meeting, the late duke's private secretary has announced to the London press that the duke's heir has been located and is delighted to be inheriting the title." He gave me a sidelong warning look.

"Yeah. Sure. I'm positively ecstatic. Can't you tell?" I laughed. "No? Must be my stuffy British side coming through."

He slid into the car. "The same announcement was sent to the Seattle press and the American media. Tomorrow. Cheerio!"

Cheerio? Really?

I realized Thorne was yanking my chain.

As Thorne's car pulled away, my phone came alive. I was bombarded with texts. I was about to turn it off when Justin called.

"What's this about you being a duke?" He was laughing. "It's all over the news, Your Grace."

Overcoming disbelief and snide comments were going to be my main challenges.

"We're of the same social status here," I said, remembering one of the few things my mom had taught me about British titles and their class system. "You can call me Duke."

CHAPTER FOUR

*H*aley Riggins Feldhem had held my hand and helped me out of a puddle of chicken soup and soggy bread. The moment he'd touched my hand I'd felt that rare jolt of chemistry. My heart had raced. And I'd blushed to the roots of my pink and lavender hair. And then he'd said he could take me away from all this!

Only to bake brownies. He'd been joking. Or had he been flirting?

Damn Sally and fate's inconvenient timing! He'd been about to say something more, something profound. I saw it in his eyes. What had Riggins been about to say?

What, Riggins? What! I mentally shook my fists and fell to my knees, pleading with fate for an answer.

I rushed to the bathroom and dashed in to change back into my baker's whites. As I changed, my mind raced with all the wonderful things he might have been about to say. Like, "Haley, what a beautiful name. I've been waiting for a girl like you. One who takes my breath away."

And then he would ask me to go someplace with him. But where?

I was lacking in imagination on where exactly he would ask to take me. Where did billionaires take dates? Take me away to Saint-Tropez? Billionaires went to the French Riviera, right? I could see myself there. I would have settled, though, for coffee down the street. Like any of that was going to happen.

I coughed, choking on a puff of flour that came out of my double-breasted white baker's jacket. Yeah, I needed to do something about that. I gave my hair a quick pat, but when I returned to the dining room all that was left at his table was a twenty-dollar bill that Mary scooped up and pocketed with a triumphant grin.

The lunch rush was clearing out. The last group of Flash girls talked excitedly as they headed for the door.

"Can you believe it?" one of them said. "Riggins is the new Duke of Witham!"

I stopped short. *A duke?* I didn't know he was British.

One of the other girls nodded. "I know! It's all over social media—the first American duke. Did you see that British guy he was with? I bet he was the old duke's lawyer."

I had almost forgotten about the British guy. I'd been so distracted by Riggins when the British guy had stopped me that I'd barely heard a thing he'd said. I'd agreed to meet him tomorrow, mostly so I could escape, change, and get back out before Riggins left.

I pulled his card from my pocket and stared at it. What did a dead duke's lawyer want with me? He'd said something about an inheritance? Yep, it was right there on his card. He was a solicitor with a London firm.

With my sister Sidney being so sick and the rent due, I could use an inheritance. A big one!

At first, I'd been half inclined to believe the Brit was a scam artist or a crackpot. The city was full of them. Except that he'd been with Riggins, which gave him authenticity.

I looked at the card again and got goose bumps on my arms. A duke's lawyer was having lunch with Riggins Feldhem on the day it was announced that Riggins was a duke? Now that same lawyer wanted to meet with me?

Haha! Maybe the duke had left me something, too. Like a pile of jewels or one of his country houses. Maybe the London townhome. A girl could dream.

I grimaced. On second thought—what if Riggins and I were related? Like long-lost distant cousins or something? I shuddered. So much for my fantasies, then, of Riggins falling madly in love with me, white-knighting me, and taking me away to Saint-Tropez.

Then again, I was always dreaming of *something*. There were other billionaires in the city. Probably none that were also dukes, though. Huh. I tucked the card back into my pocket. Back to work with me. Fortunately, there was less than an hour left before closing.

Sally let us take home the day-old baked goods. Which, naturally, were always the least popular items. Unless the head baker purposefully overstocked a fave. But that rarely happened.

Sid and I never lacked for bread. Or cake. *Let them eat cake* was a favorite joke between us. In the fall and winter it was usually carrot cake, which I loved. But apparently a lot of people didn't.

Sid was my nineteen-year-old baby sis. My *adopted* baby sis. Which wouldn't have been important or mattered at all, if not for the current circumstances.

She was half Chinese, half Anglo. After my mom's cancer treatment left her infertile, my parents had adopted Sid from China when she was almost one and I was five. Her bio mom had abandoned her on the doorstep of a Chinese orphanage hours after her birth. One-child rule. What self-respecting Chinese girl could hope for future happiness when her mom's one child had the double curse of being a girl and half white?

Sid's tragic beginning had been the best thing that could have happened to our family. It sounded sappy, but she made us a complete, happy foursome. Sid was the perfect sister. Uncomplaining. Smart. Funny. Longsuffering. She and I were best friends.

I thought Sid was beautiful. Exotic. She certainly put me and my pale face to shame. Looking at her, she could almost be mistaken for being Mediterranean or Middle Eastern. Only the slight almond shape of her big, beautiful, dark, soulful eyes gave her away. I was always envious of her dark, straight hair. And told her so about a dozen times a day.

Sid was also sick. *Very* sick. Scary sick. So sick and underweight her cheekbones were prominent like a model's and her hipbones stuck out. Everything looked good on her. If only it hadn't been because she was ill and suffering. Sometimes society had it all wrong with its obsession with skinniness.

Sid had aplastic anemia. She'd been diagnosed at the start of her senior year in high school, two years after my dad died of a heart attack. Mom died when I was fourteen. Cancer. Since Dad died, it was just Sid and me living in the old family home with a couple of girlfriends who paid a bit of rent to help out.

The doctors couldn't determine why, or how, Sid had developed anemia. Sometimes it was hereditary. And sometimes it had environmental causes. It messed with her blood cell production, all the different types of blood cells, not just red blood cells like normal anemia, and suppressed her immune system.

She was on drugs for it. A bone marrow transplant would cure her. *Cure* her! Could you imagine? Some people dreamed of great wealth or fame. Or maybe power. Sid and I dreamed of a cure, a beautiful cure. Of a hero in the form a full sibling. Even a half-sibling *might* do. A bone marrow transplant from a matching full sibling could cure her. It was almost unimaginable.

Without it, she would bounce in and out of remission and have to take drugs for the rest of her life. And had a high probability of dying young. Yeah. That was why her being adopted was important.

Sometimes we let ourselves believe that a sibling existed. It wasn't beyond the realm of possibility that her mom had found someone else and gotten married and had her "one child." But with the white father? That was the dream killer. Probably not.

A half-sibling might match. But a full sib would give Sid her best shot.

I had rushed out and been tested the moment she was diagnosed, hoping against hope I would be a match even though we shared no biology. I wasn't. But I registered for the marrow registry anyway. If I could help another family...

So far, no one had matched me. Yeah, Miss Unique. And more importantly, no one had matched Sid. The medical bills were piling up and had eaten through our inheritance and the small bit of life insurance Dad had left us. I was trying to send Sid to community college. And juggle my job. And taking care of her. And worrying about her. That was really why I needed a hero. For Sid.

Sid was sitting on the couch in the living room watching TV when I got home. Our two roomies, Liz and Jasmine, were out.

Sid's eyes lit up when I walked in the door carrying the daily bag of baked goods. She looked tired and pale.

Pretty much like usual lately. Just last week we'd gotten the bad news that she was out of remission and back in the ravages of the disease. She was taking a strong course of drugs. Her five-year survival rate odds plummeted with each passing month and year that we didn't find a cure through a bone marrow match. After twenty, her odds dropped by twelve percent.

I tried not to think about the five-year survival rates. Eighty-two percent. Which dropped to seventy percent after her twentieth birthday. More than anything, that eighteen to thirty percent death rate scared the crap out of me.

"You had a duke in the bakery today! Did you see him?" She was smiling, with that signature tease in her eyes. Sid loved life more than anyone. "Riggins Feldhem from Flashionista.com, the American duke! Did he stop by for a mint brownie? Did you manage to put an aphrodisiac in it for him?"

"Chocolate is an aphrodisiac all by itself," I said. "There's enough chocolate in those brownies to make anyone horny. But that's beside the point. I don't want to sleep with him."

Sid arched an eyebrow and made a comically mocking expression of disbelief.

I laughed. "I didn't say I'm averse to the thought. But what I need is a love potion. Totally different animal. I need him to fall madly in love with me and marry me so I can get my hands on all his cash.

"So we can travel to China and find your long-lost brother or sister." I paused and studied my stylish sister. "Actually, you're more his type. If we could get *you* into the bakery—"

She laughed again. "Shut up! Yeah, I'm sure he really wants a sick girl. Plus, he's a little old, isn't he?"

"Beggars can't be choosers," I said, sounding like I remembered Mom.

"The story's all over the news. He was just selected second hottest bachelor in Seattle. Those magazine editors should be embarrassed now. They look stupid for picking Lazer Grayson. How can the first American duke, one who looks like Riggins, *not* be the hottest guy?" She held out her hand for the bag I carried. "If he could develop a British accent, he'd be even hotter."

She peeked inside the bakery bag. "What did you bring us today? Is there cake?"

"Hardly! But there are some nice bran muffins."

She rolled her eyes and wrinkled her nose. "Bran again! We never get the popular favorites." She pulled one out of the bag and peeled away the paper muffin cup. "So, the duke! Tell me all about it. Did you see him?"

I nodded and plopped onto the couch next to her. "He was in the bakery with a British guy." I told her everything, embellishing the details of my fall to make her laugh. "Now I'll have to do a load of wash."

"But are you okay?" Sid said with that worried look on her face. She was always worrying about me.

"My knees are bruised, and maybe my heart, but I'll live." I pulled the British lawyer's card out of my pocket and showed it to her. "This is odd, though. What do you think? What could he want with me? Why would he even know who I am? Did the dead duke leave me something? What could it be?"

"Millions, I hope!" She rubbed her hands together greedily and laughed.

I scrunched my mouth to one side. "Why would a dead duke leave me millions? Why would he leave me *anything*?"

Riggins

Becoming a duke was a complete media circus. The paparazzi beat me back to the office and were lying in wait at every entrance.

"Riggins! Riggins! Look this way! How does it feel to be a duke?"

Questions and mics were shoved in my face.

I smiled and waved. "Surprising."

"You didn't know you were in line for the dukedom?"

"Not a clue."

"But you must be a British citizen?"

"I am, yes." I kept walking. "I've had dual citizenship since birth."

"Will you be looking for a duchess now? The press release from the late duke's office said you're the last male Feldhem in the family line. And you're eager to create an heir."

I bit my tongue to keep from swearing and just kept smiling. Damn Thorne and the Dead Duke. Thorne hadn't been kidding when he said the Dead Duke left nothing to chance.

"Oh, sure," I said. "I'll be throwing a ball any day now and looking for a girl in a glass slipper." I posed for a few quick shots and let myself into the building.

I was an object of curiosity as I walked through the building. Silence as I approached, followed by murmurs of speculation in my wake.

I found Justin in his office.

He looked up and grinned. "I see you made it intact through the media storm out front. Glad it's you, not me for a change, my liege."

I scowled. "We haven't gotten this much attention since your surprise marriage last summer."

"Great, isn't it?" His eyes danced.

He was obviously enjoying himself. Glad someone was.

"Our stock's up three points on the news of your new dukeness."

I shook my head, hating to burst his bubble with the bad news ahead. But I need his genius working on solving my, our, problem with the Dead Duke. "Do you have a minute? I have something I need to discuss with you. I want Harry in on the discussion, too."

"If it's about moving Flash HQ to England or adding the ducal crest to our logo, then we don't need a meeting. The answer is no."

"I wish it were that simple."

Justin caught on to my serious mood. "I'll clear my schedule. Let me buzz Harry. Your office or mine?"

"Mine. I have better booze."

He grinned. "I hope we're not losing you, Riggs."

Five minutes later, Harry, Justin, and I were meeting behind closed doors in my office. Harry and I each had a stiff drink in hand. Justin had an energy drink. I recounted my meeting with Thorne in all of its ugly detail while they sat silently listening without interrupting. I had always appreciated Harry's calm presence and Justin's surprisingly mature and clear head.

"The Dead Duke, as you call him, somehow got control of fifteen percent of our stock?" Justin looked stunned and furious at the same time. His eyes were narrowed in anger. "How the hell did that happen?"

"Good question. I thought we had safeguards in place." I took a deep gulp of my drink, feeling the burn as it went down.

"What are you going to do?" Justin said. "About getting married?"

"What can I do? If I, we, can't find a way around the blackmail, I'm going to have to marry the girl. If I don't, the Dead Duke will dump the stock and ruin us. I can't...I won't let that happen. We've all worked too hard. Justin, hell, you have a baby on the way in a few weeks."

He shrugged. "I've set some cash aside. Made some good investments outside Flash. I'd find a way to get by and rebuild."

He took a deep breath and nodded toward the door. "The people out there, though, our employees, I feel a strong obligation to them. But still, Riggs. I can't ask you to marry someone and make a kid with her to save me or anyone else. You have to do what's best for you."

Justin was surprisingly naïve. What was best for me was saving Flash.

"You don't have to ask me. If there's no way out, I'll do it. If I've pegged the Dead Duke right, he has something on the girl. Something that will ruin her, too. If I refuse, she'll go down with me. I won't do that to her, either. I don't want her ruined life on my conscience."

I took a deep breath. "I don't want to be the duke. Particularly, I don't want the estate. If I can neutralize the threat, I won't have to marry. I can donate the estate to the British public so everyone can enjoy it. And marry when, and if, I want to. And produce an heir only if I want children."

"But for now, I need to prepare for the worst. And make it look like I'm complying with the duke's wishes." I turned to Harry. "I'll need an ironclad prenup. There's no reason I should share my billions when this all falls apart."

"I'm not a divorce lawyer," Harry said with a sidelong glance at Justin. "I can refer you—"

"No. This stays here, between the three of us."

"Riggins, there's nothing scandalous in a billionaire protecting his fortune. All attorneys operate under the attorney/client privilege. I know some excellent attorneys who specialize in marital law. They're very discreet."

Justin nodded his agreement. "You need the best, Duke." He grinned.

"You're enjoying this duke crap way too much." I gave him an arch look, grinned, and nodded. "All right,

Harry. As long as you act as my agent and oversee it. I'll need your legal advice."

Harry nodded.

I finished my drink and set my glass down. "I'm just buying time so I can figure a way out of this. There has to be a way out of this mess. I need you two to help me find it."

I turned to Jus. "The Dead Duke can't be as clever as he thought he was. He has to have made a mistake somewhere."

Justin nodded.

"I was caught off guard by this duke crap. I have less than twenty-four hours before I have to propose. First thing—check the financials to see if he can deliver on his threat or if he's just blowing smoke. Unfortunately, from what Thorne showed me, I think it's a long shot that he's bluffing. I think the threat is genuine."

"I'm in. We'll work it together," Justin said.

"I'll take a look at the legal documents and get some help on British law from my connections in London," Harry said.

I nodded. "Good. Between the three of us, we should be able to defeat the duke." I paused. "Who knew a dead guy could wield so much power?"

"Something to strive for." Justin finished his energy drink and grinned. "Power from beyond the grave," he said in a deep announcer voice.

I took another long breath. "In the meantime, I have to propose to this girl tomorrow at Thorne's rented temporary office. Either of you two have any suggestions?"

"'Will you marry me?' is to the point and pretty standard." Harry finished his drink and set the glass down on the bar.

"Justin? How did you propose?" I was curious. Justin had never said.

"The hell if I know." He shot a glance at Harry again. "I don't remember. I was drunk."

"Such a romantic." I shook my head at them. "You two are no help."

"Now that you're British and a duke, you could go more formal and flowery," Justin said. "Try something classically British, like, 'I love you tragically. Would you do me the honor of accepting my hand?'"

"That sounds like something you'd hear in a PBS British drama," Harry said. "Masterpiece Classic. Or a BBC production."

"Exactly! That's what I was going for." Justin looked pleased with himself.

I looked heavenward. But no help was forthcoming.

Haley

Sid worried over me as I got ready for my appointment with the British lawyer. "Should you go alone? Maybe I should go with you?"

"I don't think he's dangerous," I said. "We're meeting in a private conference room at one of those places downtown where you can rent office space for a few hours at a time. It's very public and safe."

Sid frowned. "Yes, but maybe you should have a lawyer with you?"

I shook my head. "Why would I need a lawyer? Just because he's one? I don't think so. Besides, we can't afford one. So, moot point."

"I would still feel better if you took someone with you. I could call Sam. He's big and tough and can beat the crap out of this British dude if he tries to hurt you."

Sam was her friend and sometimes boyfriend.

I shook my head more vigorously. "Look, if it makes you feel any better, I'm a complete skeptic. I'm not easily conned. And I'll bring my panther claw self-defense keychain. Will that make you happy?"

"No." She smiled sweetly.

I rolled my eyes and hugged her goodbye.

I caught the bus downtown. I'd dressed casually for this meeting in jeans, a cute blouse, tennies, and a sweater cape that Sid had bought off Flashionista for me, insisting I should pay some attention to being stylish. She loved shopping on Flashionista. Which partially explained her fascination with Riggins. It was her dream to work there someday after she got her degree.

The offices I was meeting Mr. Thorne at were just a block off the bus line with a view of the sound. It was a brisk, windy day in downtown Seattle. Not at all unusual for the time of year. Cloudy, but no rain.

I arrived right on time and checked in with the receptionist at the front desk.

"Mr. Thorne is waiting for you." She showed me to a conference room at the back of building. It wasn't anything spectacular, but the view was nice.

The receptionist knocked on the door and let me in. "Miss Hamilton, sir."

Mr. Thorne was seated, waiting for me and drinking a cup of tea. He got to his feet and extended his hand. "Miss Hamilton. Right on time. Thank you for coming. I appreciate your time."

I shook his hand, heart pounding with anticipation and a fair amount of fear. Even though I had tried not to, I had set my expectations too high. I wanted money and hoped dollar signs weren't shining in my eyes.

"Good to see you again. You were mysterious yesterday. You said you had something important to discuss with me?"

"I do. Please, be seated." He offered me a chair. "Can I offer you something to drink? Coffee? Tea? Water?"

"No, thank you. I'm fine." I was too nervous to drink anything and eager to get to the heart of the matter.

"Very good." His briefcase sat on the conference table in front of him. "Shall we get down to business, then?"

I nodded and smiled, trying not to cross my fingers.

He opened the briefcase and pulled out a sheaf of papers. "How much do you know about your family history, Miss Hamilton?"

I shrugged. "Not much. I know my grandparents' names, but I couldn't tell you who my great grandparents were. I'm not into genealogy. It never seemed important. My sister is adopted. She doesn't know anything about her biological family."

Which was a big part of our problem.

"Blood family isn't that important to me, not in that way. Family is who you make it. Who you grew up with and who you love.

"With Sid not knowing where she came from, it seemed rude and uncool to be too into mine. Like she wasn't really part of ours."

He let me speak, wearing a calm, masked expression that didn't give his opinions away. "I see. You are unaware, then, of your ancestry?"

"That's right."

"I represent the late Duke of Witham. He didn't share your opinion about family. Bloodlines were exceptionally important to him."

I nodded, trying to figure out where this was going.

"As you may have heard on the news, the late duke had no children. No sons to inherit his title. That being the case, the title went to Mr. Riggins Feldhem, a distant cousin of the late duke."

I kept nodding like a bobblehead doll, wondering where this was going. And how I was going to benefit from the duke's death. There didn't seem to be any connection. If I had any British ancestry, it was way back in my family line. As far as I knew, I was a good old American mutt. Part this and part that.

"The late duke married three times, trying to have an heir. Sadly, all three wives predeceased him and left no living issue."

I raised an eyebrow. "He sounds like a Henry the VIII type."

Mr. Thorne smiled. "Not exactly, no. All of his wives died of natural causes."

I nodded, trying to look sympathetic. "He was very old, though, wasn't he? The news said a hundred and five? Any children would have been old, too."

Mr. Thorne nodded. "Yes, exactly so. No children. No grandchildren. No direct descendants."

"Too bad for the old man."

"Yes, very," Mr. Thorne said. "He had a particular affection for his first wife, Helen. She was an American heiress. Tragically, she died in childbirth, giving birth to His Grace's only son. Who passed away of a childhood fever a few years later."

"That's sad," I said, still wondering where all this was going.

"Yes, indeed it was." Mr. Thorne studied me. "Would it surprise you to learn that Helen was your great-aunt—several greats, actually?" He slid one of the papers in front of me, showing me a genealogy chart that linked me to her.

"Really?" I pulled the chart toward me for a better look. Now I *was* interested. Maybe the duke had left Sid and me a little money after all. Or a family heirloom that had been Helen's. Something I could sell for a good enough price to help Sid.

Mr. Thorne nodded. "Yes. Helen was not only the duke's favorite wife, she was the only one to produce a child." He paused as if looking for the right words. "I'm not quite sure how to present this to you, Miss Hamilton—"

"Please, call me Haley."

He nodded. "Haley. The late duke was obsessed with continuing his bloodline after his death and ensuring the title didn't go extinct."

He explained about extant—meaning the title was still in existence—and extinct titles.

"It was the great tragedy of his life that he hadn't protected the dukedom by providing an heir. The new duke is the last male in the Feldhem line." He paused significantly again. "He is obligated to take the title and do his best to provide an heir."

I almost laughed. Was having a lot of sex really such a bad deal for a guy? Wow, onerous chore! It wasn't like *he* was going to be the one who got sick and pregnant and had to waddle around for months.

I stared at Mr. Thorne, thinking Riggins would have no problem finding any number of beautiful women lining up to be his duchess and volunteering to produce dozens of beautiful heirs and spares. The entertainment news shows were already speculating about a certain lingerie model he'd taken to a few high-profile events. But what did that have to do with me?

"You are the last female of childbearing age in Helen's line. The late duke's last wish was for his line to merge with Helen's to provide the heir they should have had together." He gave me a serious, significant look.

My heart stopped. My hands went to ice. I stared at Mr. Thorne. I looked around the room like he might be talking to someone else. Maybe that gorgeous lingerie model. But nope. There was just me. "What are you saying?"

Okay, I was being dense. But who wouldn't be?

"The late duke hand-selected you, Haley, to be the new duchess. He wants you to marry the new duke and produce an heir."

My mouth fell open. I started laughing. Yes, I'd had my little crush on Riggins. But I couldn't picture myself with him in real life.

"That's ridiculous! Does Riggins know about this? Doesn't *he* have a say in it?"

Mr. Thorne wasn't laughing. He obviously didn't see the humor in the situation.

"He does, indeed. He has agreed to fulfill the late duke's wishes. Provided, of course, that you agree, too."

Okay, just when my heart had started beating again, his words stopped it up short. I shook my head, trying to knock some sense into what I was hearing. "He wants to marry *me*?"

"Want may be a bit strong. But he is willing, yes."

"Well, there's a ringing endorsement." I didn't even try to keep the sarcasm out of my voice. I had set my purse on the table. I grabbed it now, ready to bolt. "This *has* to be a joke. It's ridiculous. If it's for real, it's positively medieval."

I pushed back from the table. "I'm not ready to get married. And even if I were, I'm not marrying some guy who's being forced to marry me. We don't do arranged marriages here."

"The late duke is prepared to make it worth your while. His estate will pay you handsomely."

I shook my head vehemently. "To make a baby with a guy who's not in love with me? No way. No thank you. There's nothing that would entice me—"

"Your sister is sick, is she not?"

Except maybe that. I hesitated and swallowed against my suddenly dry mouth. How much did he know about me?

"I'm talking about a *great* deal of money. Nearly a hundred and fifty million in American dollars. Along with access to the late duke's connections in China and his web of private investigators."

I fell back into my chair, feeling almost faint. Or maybe it was giddy.

"Your sister has aplastic anemia. She needs expensive drugs to maintain her health and force her back into remission. A bone marrow transplant from a full sibling would cure her, would it not?"

I didn't answer. I couldn't. My mind was full and racing. But my voice had temporarily failed me.

Mr. Thorne glanced at his cell phone and sent a quick text. "The late duke's estate can provide for her. And help you search. If there's a sibling, or a match from a non-related stranger, anywhere in the world, we can help you find it."

He paused for dramatic emphasis. "Would you close the doors on your sister's hope for a cure so easily?"

CHAPTER FIVE

Riggins

Nothing. Damn it. *Nothing.*

Justin and I stayed up most of the night. The Dead Duke's investments were legit. He could ruin us. Legally, legitimately take everything we'd worked for. All the wealth I'd built. I would still be the duke. The Broke Duke. Which didn't have quite the same ring to it as the Billionaire Duke the media had dubbed me.

I would have access to enough money to maintain Witham House, austerely. With the stipulation that I live in the estate and manage it.

All of the money from his mother that was separate from the estate, most of which was currently invested in Flash so he could ruin me, would be donated to charity. I would lose my freedom and be a slave to a dukedom I had no love or affinity for.

On the other hand, if I married Haley, I would lose my bachelorhood and freedom, too. But only temporarily. I was sure she and I could work out an arrangement. Partner to defeat the Dead Duke and get our freedom back. Barring that, worst-case scenario, produce an heir and a spare and divorce. Or simply look the other way and ignore each other's infidelities. Wasn't that the way these aristocratic marriages worked?

As for me, I had never been more popular. Nearly every woman I'd ever dated had used some form of social media to congratulate me on my inheritance. And tell me they would just love to see me again and hear all the details.

That was the women I knew. Complete strangers had bombarded the Flash customer service lines trying to get in touch with me. I was going to have to give my customer service reps on the front lines a bonus for the work they were doing. In the meantime, real customers were becoming irritated with the delays and my social media accounts were overwhelmed.

I was just about to open up the Billionaire Duke Hotline. *Are you a single woman? Want a shot at a title? Call in toll free at 1-800-GET-DUKE to register for your chance.*

Just before eleven, I sat in the lobby of the rented offices and waited for Thorne to text me confirmation that Haley had agreed to the Dead Duke's terms. I was fairly certain he would be tempting her with half of the

Dead Duke's mother's money—half of three hundred million dollars. How could she turn that down?

I had my work cut out for me. Convincing her to walk away from that kind of money? I must have been crazy. I probably was. That damn Dead Duke had thwarted the most obvious move—make myself undesirable to her.

If I knew my adversary as I was beginning to, he had more leverage on her. He hadn't lived over a century without becoming as cunning as an old vampire.

I'd stalked Haley. On social media. Looking for deal breakers. Anything I could use to get out of this match. Something I could point to that marked her as unacceptable in the Dead Duke's terms. Like infertility. That would pretty much rule her out.

Though how the hell I could tell anything about her fertility without access to her medical records was beyond me. And even if I could get to her records, why would she have been tested for fertility issues?

I didn't find anything obvious. She had a pretty adopted sister. Her parents were dead. No in-laws to deal with. No pain in the butt mother-in-law. No father to ask permission. That was something.

She was ten years younger than I was. Without much money, from what I could tell. She'd graduated from the University of Washington with a business degree. Then promptly ignored her degree and gone to pastry school. She'd worked at The Blackberry Bakery for just over a year.

Her friends looked young. Her tastes ran young. She seemed young. Nothing I found out about her gave me any confidence we were a good match. I shoved my physical reaction to her yesterday out of my mind. The Dead Duke obviously hadn't been concerned about the ten traits of compatibility when he'd decided on pairing us.

His love of his first wife's bloodline was certainly loyal. Some might even say sweet and romantic. *Shit.*

I got a text from Thorne. *Just a few more minutes.*

Crap. How hard was he twisting the poor girl's arm? Once I made my case, I hoped she'd see that being allied with me was the smarter choice.

Haley

"All right. I'll do it." I made a split-second, gut-reaction decision. Anything for Sid. Being a duchess married to a hot billionaire wouldn't exactly be the worst hardship in the world, would it?

The part about having a baby, though...

Anything for Sid! This was Sid's life we were talking about. She would love a little niece or nephew. And I wanted her to be around for one for a long, long time.

"But I want the terms spelled out. In a legal document." I eyed Mr. Thorne suspiciously. "I guess you would call it a prenup. I want everything in writing, including the exact terms I need to fulfill to get the money. And what will happen in the case of a divorce. I'm sure I'm going to want to keep my baby."

I would need a lawyer. But was this even legal?

"Naturally."

"I'll want my own lawyer to go over it."

"Of course. Very prudent of you." Mr. Thorne looked slightly relieved. "I'll draw up the documents. When they're ready, you can forward them to your lawyer."

"Okay." I slumped in the chair. "What happens next?"

"I call the duke in. He's waiting in the lobby. He has something to ask you."

Riggins

Thorne texted me again. *We're ready for you. Please join us. Haley is amenable to your upcoming proposal.*

Great. This wasn't exactly how I imagined proposing to a woman. I hadn't even contacted my friends in the diamond business. But you did what you had to do. And then found a workaround. An escape hatch.

Thorne stood when I entered the room. "Your Grace."

I didn't think I would ever get used to being called that. "Thorne."

He wore his usual impeccable manners. Haley sat in a chair in front of a conference table, looking small and uncertain. She was dressed casually, clearly not expecting a marriage proposal. Or to have her life upended.

My heart clenched at the sight of her. Wearing makeup and street clothes, with her hair tumbling over her shoulders, she was even cuter than she'd been yesterday. I had the unreasonable, crazy urge to protect her. She brought out that long-dead instinct in me. Maybe it had just been lying fallow. Yeah, Riggins

Feldhem, protector of the innocent. And douche who proposed to women he wasn't in love with. The fact that I was doing it under duress made no difference to my conscience.

I smiled at her, trying to reassure her. Or myself. I wasn't exactly sure. Maybe both of us. "Haley."

"Your Grace," she said uncertainly. But her eyes danced with devilment. She was teasing me, like Justin had.

I turned to Thorne, my new expert on all things ducal. "Does she have to call me that? Isn't she my equal?"

Thorne smiled. "Not yet, Your Grace."

Now he was just rubbing it in. And trying not to laugh. I didn't miss the corners of his lips trying to turn up. So maybe old Thorne had a droll, very dry sense of humor.

"Miss Hamilton is still a commoner, not an aristocrat, until you make her your duchess." He pulled an antique ring box from his pocket and held it out to me, balanced on his palm.

Haley blushed and looked away, biting her lip, and looking very young and vulnerable. And uncomfortable.

I felt like shit putting her in this situation. Even though I wasn't the villain here. Thorne should have been the one with the guilty conscience. But he looked perfectly calm.

The Dead Duke had no shame. He was dead, after all. And probably rotting in hell for all his evil machinations. You couldn't tell me we were the first two people he'd ever manipulated. If he was so damned good at it from the grave, I had no doubt he'd had plenty of practice in life.

Thorne was still holding the ring box out to me. Haley still looked away. See no ring. Hear no conspiring and no coercing.

A woman should be romanced. Her marriage proposal shouldn't shatter her dreams, but make them fly. Just because Prince William gave Princess Kate, the Duchess of Cambridge, his late mother's ring didn't mean my bride should be stuck with an antique ring that wasn't her style. Was it her style? I had no idea.

This was an insufferable, unconscionable way to go into a marriage. I wasn't about to shatter her romantic dreams this way. "I can't do it."

Thorne's eyebrows rose with surprise.

Haley finally turned to face me, lips trembling. Tears in her eyes. "But you have to. *We* have to."

Was she actually begging me to propose to her? What had Thorne blackmailed her with?

"I'm not backing out of the agreement. But I can't propose like this," I said, sounding like the romantic I wasn't. "In an office. After a lawyer has just handed me a ring I haven't seen yet. It's not right."

I smiled at Haley again, suddenly playing knight valiant. I knelt down next to her. "It's not the fairytale either of us want. Public opinion will crucify us if they smell any hint of an arranged marriage. It's not the American way. We like our romance and our passion."

"May I remind, Your Grace, that you are British?"

I ignored Thorne. I had a sudden brilliant idea. A very public romance. A Cinderella story played out before the media's eyes.

"The media loves me right now." I flashed Haley a quick grin. "They love the idea of a duke looking for a bride. A whirlwind romance? A Cinderella story!" I nodded, agreeing with myself.

I stood up and fell into the chair opposite Haley. I took both of her icy hands in mine and squeezed them. "You can be that Cinderella. You can be *my* Cinderella. A true duchess. It will be genuine rags to riches." I gave her hands another squeeze and stared into her eyes. "Well? What do you say?"

"Yes. All right." She nodded as the wheels of her mind turned. "Okay, so we're telling a story. Creating an image. Feeding a fantasy."

"Exactly!" Buying ourselves time to get out of this mess. Sending business Flash's direction. Fortifying my brand so the Dead Duke couldn't destroy it.

When she smiled, it lit her whole face and transformed her. The insecurity was gone. She had beautiful dimples and full, wide lips. She had a gorgeous, genuine smile. I liked a woman who could smile. I felt unexpectedly tender towards her. There was that thing about her again, that dangerous thing, that reminded me of being young and in love.

"When do we start?" she said.

"As soon as we walk out of this room." I stood and snatched the ring box from Thorne's hand. "The story is simple. We met at the American reading of the Dead Duke's will. He left you a few trinkets—"

"More like millions." She laughed. "*If* I comply with his wishes. In any fairytale, there's always a catch, isn't there?"

I liked her. She had some spunk. Properly cultivated...

I turned to Thorne. "In the meantime, is there something the Dead Duke can leave her?

"Certainly, Your Grace. Something from her great-aunt, perhaps. Something worth a few thousand pounds can be found, I'm sure."

I nodded. "Good."

I looked at Haley again. "Back to our story. We hit it off immediately. Went out to coffee after our meeting with Thorne—"

"No. I'm sorry, but you're wrong, Your Grace." Her eyes danced.

"Please, call me duke."

She laughed. "I would prefer Riggins."

"Riggins, then." I grinned at her. "How am I wrong?"

She raised one eyebrow. "We met at the bakery. Where I worked horrendously hard in the back, hefting heavy trays of baked goods into ovens and slaving over the heat for eight hours a day. Like a true Cinderella. Because everyone knows that the way to a man's heart is through his stomach—"

"That's a cliché," I said.

She ignored me. "I baked your favorite mint brownies day after day, drawing you into the bakery with the tantalizing twin thoughts of chocolate and mint. You caught glimpses of me from time to time, which piqued your interest. Something about a girl in a uniform."

She was clearly enjoying teasing.

"You longed for me, almost tragically." She winked at me.

The woman was yanking my chain. And she knew it. But damn, I liked a woman with wit.

"Of course, you were intrigued," she continued. "Who wouldn't be? Running with the cliché, as you call it, there's nothing quite as sexy as a girl in baker's whites who smells like cinnamon, vanilla, mint, and chocolate—"

"And wears flour on her nose," I added.

"It's cheaper, pound for pound, than face powder. And more nutritious. So there's that." She kept smiling that infectious smile. "But fate conspired against us. Until one day, the bakery was short on waitstaff. And this junior baker had to fill in. She was accidentally tripped by an oblivious patron, fell to the floor with a clatter of dishes, and you white-knighted her, helping her out of an embarrassing situation."

"White-knighted?" I said.

She kept smiling. "Our eyes met. We felt an instant connection. We were soul mates who might never have met except for an accident, a bit of clumsiness, and the death of a distant relative.

"When we met again at the reading of his will, we both had a good laugh at the coincidence. And admitted that fate must be guiding us toward each other. *Then* we pick up with your story. You may ask me to coffee now." Her eyes twinkled.

I wasn't usually socially inept. But I'd made a tactical mistake in forgetting that public incident. No woman wants to think she's forgettable. Or worse, invisible. I nodded. "You're right. My apologies. Our story began earlier. I'll ask you for coffee as we're walking out. On the spur of the moment. Completely naturally. In the lobby in front of the receptionist, where we can be sure the most people will be likely to hear. And spread the word. We have to be seen."

"Oh, of course. I can be a media whore." Her smile was simply dazzling.

Thorne cleared his throat. "May I remind you? There is a deadline for the nuptials to take place. The late duke was not a patient man. Even in death. I would advise you not to try his patience, or you may find the generous terms of his offer are withdrawn. With dire consequences."

Ah, the veiled threat. Very effective.

I studied Thorne. He wasn't bluffing. But neither did I believe the Dead Duke would let us go. I was positive he had something up his sleeve to push us into action. Merely giving up and ruining us wouldn't accomplish his objective.

"Oh, come on, Thorne! Don't be such a stick in the mud. We deserve a *little* time to get to know each other. And the public deserves their fairytale romance. In a few weeks, everyone will believe we're so in love, that we can't wait to marry. If we play it right, we can become famous for no real reason at all. In the big scheme, what's a fortnight?" I was throwing in a little British to throw him off and make him comfortable.

Haley backed me up. "We'll merge our bloodlines soon enough." She gave me a questioning look.

I laughed uncomfortably. "Thorne explained to me. You're a descendent of the Dead Duke's first wife?"

"Yes. Dear old auntie." She stood, too. "It's fate. Kismet. Two unlikely lovers meet in sad circumstances. Two great bloodlines collide again in true love."

She paused. "Your DNA yearns for mine. *Ardently.*" She laughed. "Be sure to use *ardently* when you propose. I like that word. It's very British. Very Mr. Darcy."

I nodded. "As long as it's in a public place. With the eyes of the world on us."

She clasped her hands in front of her chest. "My knight in shining armor."

I was beginning to enjoy myself. I slid the ring box into my pocket without looking at it.

"I hate to interject business into this lighthearted conversation about faking love," I said, "but I'll need you to sign a prenup."

She nodded. "Naturally. I expected nothing less. You'd be a dumb businessman not to. I don't like stupid men."

I liked her more and more. "Just so we're clear. You won't get *any* of my assets."

She seemed too calm and casual about it.

She shrugged again. "I stand to inherit over one hundred million. Keep your billions. I won't need them. And just so we're clear, I'll need *you* to sign a prenup, too."

I looked at her, startled. What could she *possibly* have that I would want part of?

She read the question on my face. "I get custody of any child or children we create. I promise to raise him, or her, in the most appropriately dukely fashion an American duchess can possibly manage. But the child is mine."

"You want me to give up my firstborn? You know you sound a lot like you're rehearsing a scene from *Into the Woods*?" I raised an eyebrow now, amused. And impressed. She had guts *and* she liked kids.

If I was going to be saddled with a wife, those were two good traits for her to have.

"Not just *our* firstborn. *Our* second and third, if that's what it takes to produce an heir. I get sole custody of *all* the progeny we make. And I will insist on child support for them. A father should contribute to their care. Even if I don't personally need it."

"Joint custody," I said, with no room for negotiation.

The whole point was moot. We weren't having *any* children together. We weren't getting married. Not if I could help it.

But if I had to be stuck with someone in this situation, she seemed like a good ally. Smart. Adventurous. Sharp enough to help me break the Dead Duke's impossible blackmail demands?

Even though there weren't going to be any children, *she* didn't know that yet. She had no idea what my intentions were.

I didn't want to look like a deadbeat douchebag. The kind of guy who wouldn't care about his children. If there were any children, I wouldn't be an absentee dad, like mine had been. That was a bunch of crap and damaged a child's psyche. So I put up a fight, partly for show. Partly to test her.

Her eyes narrowed as she studied me. She was obviously primed for battle. But there was admiration there, too. Finally she broke into a smile, like I had passed some kind of test. "Good! I wouldn't marry any guy who wouldn't fight for his kids. No matter how much I was coerced." She slid a glance at Thorne.

"It's all settled, then," Thorne said. "Everyone gets their lawyers to put the appropriate paperwork together. You two conduct a showy, *short* public romance, and everyone lives happily ever after. Just like in the storybooks."

Haley and I rolled our eyes and grinned at each other.

"Splendid!" Thorne said. "We'll reconvene in, let's say, a week? And get all the paperwork out of the way."

CHAPTER SIX

*H*aley *That went absurdly*, I thought as I walked out of Thorne's rented office with Riggins. *I'm going to be a duchess? Riggins' duchess?* I kept expecting to wake up. *Someone pinch me.*

Riggins was ten years older than I was, but ridiculously hot. And rich. Which didn't really matter now, did it? I was going to be wealthy in my own right. And take care of Sid. And find her cure. One way or the other. And then the two of us, Sid and I, would be set for life. And we could help others. Or do whatever we wanted. After this little episode and adventure with Riggins ended.

I pushed all the uncomfortable thoughts about marrying a man I didn't know aside as we strolled through the lobby, laughing and joking with each other, putting on a show. Chatting with him, teasing him, even almost flirting with him, felt amazingly natural and easy. It shouldn't have. But it did. That was a good sign.

We drew attention. More accurately, Riggins drew attention. No one cared about me. He was a local celebrity. The second hottest, most eligible bachelor in the city. People were trying not to gawk. But who wouldn't? How many hot billionaires did you see in everyday life?

"Haley?" he said as we reached the reception desk and the door.

He spoke in a voice that was just loud enough to be heard by the general vicinity. But not loud enough to be obviously loud and a plea for attention.

"Do you have to run?" His smile made me go soft in the knees.

I opened my mouth but no sound came out. I was dazzled. Star-struck. My pulse raced. I shook my head. So much for talking with him being easy. It was more like a rollercoaster ride.

"Excellent." His face lit up.

If only it were real.

"Let me buy you a cup of coffee?"

I nodded. First date, coffee date. I approved. On many levels, I was a simple girl. In my opinion, one of the must-do dates for every relationship was the basic, low-pressure coffee date. Though I doubted this public viewing would be anything other than stressful. Still, the thought was there.

I loved it when a guy wanted to get to know me first. Especially before an arranged marriage—haha. But, in general, if a coffee date went badly, no one had wasted much time, money, or effort. It was an easy way to see if there was any spark, any chance of a real relationship. Of course, in our case, we were going to have to proceed no matter what. Lack of chemistry or dark of night, nothing stopped the Dead Duke's maniacal marriage plans for us!

Riggins took my arm. "I know of a little place just around the corner."

He guided me outside, his hand still on my arm. And so warm and obvious there was no way I could ignore it.

He glanced back at the office building as we walked away, and leaned in close to me. "Good job! People were definitely listening. I think they bought our act."

Had they? I hadn't been paying attention. His nearness rattled me. I couldn't think of anything stellar to say. "So. Where are we going for coffee?"

Now that was brilliant, sparkling conversation. Yes, I could take the prize when I tried.

He smelled *delicious*. Scrumptious in a clean, sexy, masculine way. I would have asked him what cologne he was wearing, but I felt shy and the question seemed suddenly personal and probably out of the blue.

"Just around the corner." His voice was deep and sexy, smooth and sophisticated. "To the right."

Next to him I felt young and awkward. He was dressed in stylish, expensive clothes. I was dressed in jeans. I looked nice. *For me.*

But who could have predicted I was going to a lawyer's office to catch a husband and come out a duchess-to-be? I was hoping for an antique ring. Not an antique engagement ring. It was practically like being a princess. And just as surreal.

Riggins smiled at me and gave me an appreciative up-and-down. "I like your cape."

A compliment! Not as good as "you are devastatingly beautiful and take my breath away," but good enough. I liked compliments. Who didn't? Maybe now I should compliment his cologne...

"We sold one like it recently."

Oh. I see.

"Thanks." My voice was flat. "My sister bought it for me. From Flashionista." I rambled at the worst times. "She's a huge fan."

So it was only my clothes he was appreciating. And even then, only in a professional manner. As in, his company had made a sale. Maybe he'd been admiring the fact that I patronized his company. And I'd just blown it by confessing Sid was the fan, not necessarily me.

Sid! She would laugh so hard about me becoming a duchess. And the wife of Flashionista's biggest shareholder. If I hadn't been next to Riggins, I would have rubbed my hands together evilly. Now there would be no stopping Sid if she still wanted a job there after my marriage. Nepotism and all that.

Riggins and I walked side by side to the coffee shop, The Taste Test. I'd actually been to it once. It was locally owned. Not a ubiquitous chain. One of those places that made every single beverage they served by hand. They measured, frothed, and heated the milk individually for each drink, rather than in batches. So each batch of frothed milk was entirely fresh. No scummy old milk skins in any of their drinks.

They made all their own syrups from scratch—the whiskey-caramel sauce, the hazelnut puree, the dark fudge sauce. It was heaven, really. Nothing here was prepackaged or premade. All natural. Organic if possible. Freshly made. They bought their pastries from several sources, including the Blackberry. Because of our "freshly baked daily from scratch" policy and commitment to using high-quality, locally sourced ingredients.

Riggins put his large hand in the small of my back as he ushered me in the door. It felt possessive and intimate. And scorched where it rested.

There was something about a guy with big hands. Was I right? I was *hyper*aware of him.

The counter, pastry case, and coffee kitchen were in an island in the middle of shop. The menu hung in the middle behind the serving counter. We stood side by side, staring at it in awkward silence.

"Everything's good here," Riggins said, finally. He smiled at me and I thought I might melt.

This was dangerous territory. I was an impressionable girl who'd been looking for a hero for too long. And now, totally against his will, Riggins was looking more and more like one. Or maybe the Dead Duke was. Anyway, Riggins was my ticket to everything I wanted and needed. Being with him could save Sid.

The guy behind the counter was probably late twenties, and friendly. "What can I get for you today?"

A server leaned in and whispered a question to him. From the way the staff deferred to him, he had to be one of the owners.

On another day, I would have noticed him. He was cute and he wasn't wearing a ring. I might even have flirted. But he paled in comparison to Riggins. I realized with a start that I was suddenly a taken woman.

Riggins deferred to me.

"I'd like a macchiato. Can you make it with whiskey-caramel sauce?"

The guy behind the counter grinned, proud of his place. "We can make it any way you want." He held up two cups in two different sizes.

"Small." My eye wandered over the pastry case as Riggins ordered a hazelnut mocha. I recognized some of the Blackberry's baked goods.

"We make those!" I pointed to a tray of scones. "I'm a baker at the Blackberry."

"We love the Blackberry!" The guy behind the counter lit up. "And we love your mission. The other owner, my business partner, has years of culinary training and experience. If we had the facilities, she would do our baking. But you guys are great. She has great respect for your baking."

"That's awesome!" I said.

We broke into an animated discussion about baking philosophies. Until Riggins politely cleared his throat.

"Sorry." Cute guy smiled apologetically. "Name for the order?"

"Riggins." Riggins cast a quick glance at me. As we walked away from the counter, he whispered to me, "Were you flirting with that guy? Right in front of your soon-to-be fiancé?"

The warmth of his voice made my heart soar. The complete lack of any jealousy was somewhat alarming, though.

"Absolutely not. Just talking shop with a fellow professional and enthusiast."

"So that's what you call it?"

I rolled my eyes at him. "You should have given your name for the order as the Duke of Witham. That would have scared him off."

We took a seat at an intimate two-person table by the window. Maximum visibility.

Riggins grinned. "You think he would have been impressed?"

"He would have expected a bigger tip, that's for sure." I grinned at Riggins. He was way too easy on the eyes.

And speaking of eyes, his were dark and expressive. The corners around them creased when he smiled, and made him look rugged.

"You don't tip the owner of an establishment," he said.

The coffee shop was busy, and hummed with the white noise of dozens of voices talking. The buzz and thrum made eavesdropping on other conversations difficult at best. Which was good for us. We were cloaked in relative conversation privacy. We drew a few interested stares, but people were too polite to approach us. Riggins seemed oblivious to the looks and whispers. I assumed he was used to them. They both fascinated and frightened me.

Riggins leaned across the table, staring deep into my eyes. My heart raced wildly and unevenly and the world spun slowly. I could melt in a gaze like that. In fact, I was. Or, at the very least, I was slumping.

I reminded myself to sit up straight. Future duchesses never let their backs touch the back of chairs. I think that admonishment generally applied to all aristocratic ladies.

Riggins spoke in a low, intimate tone that could turn a girl like me to jelly. "How the hell are we going to get out of this marriage? What does that damned Dead Duke have on you?"

Way to shatter the illusion, Duke.

Before I could answer, the barista called Riggins' name and set our order on the counter. We both rose out of our chairs. The automatic waitress in me.

Riggins motioned me back down. "I'll get it."

"Don't trust my waitressing skills?" I tried to sound flippant and flirty.

He grinned and went to the counter. The barista had filled the cups to the very top, so full that only surface tension kept them from spilling over. That was a common trick. Small cups filled to the top made the patron feel like he was getting his money's worth.

I almost laughed as I watched Riggins walk very slowly and carefully back to our table, trying not to slosh our coffee. I think I would have laughed if my heart hadn't been broken by his immediate desire to get out of marrying me. So much for my vanity.

"Waitressing isn't as easy as I make it look, is it?" I teased.

"The cups are too full." He grinned back at me.

"Excuses, excuses."

He set my coffee in front of me and his in front of him.

Baristas in shops like this one considered themselves artists in milk frothery. The barista had made a heart pattern in the foam of each of our cups. A little heart in my smaller cup. A bigger one in Riggins'. What a cute matched set!

I pointed to our cups and leaned in to Riggins. "Our act is working already. The barista thinks we're lovebirds."

"Or it could be because it's close to Valentine's Day." He raised an eyebrow.

I laughed. "Killjoy."

Riggins laughed, too, and made a point of giving me another intense, almost adoring look as he took a sip of his coffee, destroying both the coffee heart and mine. He was a master of that seductive expression.

Experienced, I thought. Way more than I was. If I'd been given three wishes, I would have used one wishing for sophistication.

I matched his expression, looking at him with awe and adoration. Or trying to, at least.

"You were saying?" I said, coolly, trying out a duchess-like voice. Without the British accent.

"What does the Dead Duke have on you?" he repeated. "And don't play coy with me. I know he has *something*. The Dead Duke left nothing to chance. Or so I've been told."

I hesitated, wondering how much to reveal. As far as I remembered, there was no nondisclosure attached to my inheritance. I took a minute to collect my thoughts and didn't answer immediately.

Riggins stepped in, filling the void in conversation. "I'll tell you what he's using against me. He's blackmailing me. Threatening to ruin me if I don't 'sire an heir.'"

Riggins glanced out the window as calmly as if he'd been talking about the weather. His gaze returned to me. "With you. After a lawful wedding. Bastard children can't inherit."

A tall, thin, beautiful woman was walking by. I jealously wondered if she had been what had caught his attention.

"That sounds very old-fashioned," I said. "Siring, I mean."

"It's archaic. Despicable. I wouldn't agree to his terms without coercing." He studied me. "You aren't curious how he's blackmailing me?"

I shrugged. I was dying to know. I figured that sooner or later it would come out. "It's your business."

His smile deepened. He liked my answer. "So? You?"

There was no reason to hide it from him. He could easily find out anyway.

"My sister is sick." I explained about Sid. Told him the whole longwinded story. "He can help."

Riggins nodded. "I have money. *I* can help."

"You would pay me *not* to marry you?" I asked, looking at him pointedly. My vanity was almost fatally wounded now, limping along on its last legs. Not that I should have been surprised.

He studied me. "There's something you should know. But before I can tell you, you have to swear not to tell anyone. Ever."

"Intriguing," I said.

He arched an eyebrow. "It's important and affects you."

"Well, then. What can I do? Your secret is safe with me."

He smiled softly and stared into his coffee before looking up at me with a heart-melting, earnest look. "I don't want to be duke. I don't want the estate. I'm trying to find a way out. I won't stop until I do."

He paused. "I thought you should know. Before you marry me. If I have my way, one of two things will happen—either you won't be a duchess long. Or you won't be a duchess of much long. Not more than a duchess in title only."

He leaned forward and took my hand that had been resting on the table. His was warm. His touch distracted my thoughts.

"If I'm going to pull this off, I need your help. If we work together, we can defeat the Dead Duke and not have to marry at all."

I tried not to look devastated, or even crestfallen.

He squeezed my hand. "It's nothing personal. I'm sure you'd make a great duchess." His tone was genuine and kind. And heartbreaking. "You'll also be the perfect ally. No one else will do."

I hadn't realized how much I'd glommed onto the idea of being his duchess. "I'm the last woman of childbearing age in my line. I'm worth a lot to the deceased His Grace." I stared Riggins down, wondering if I could trust him. Wondering how mercenary and greedy I really was at heart.

There was a lot of money at stake. A mind-boggling amount. More than I needed, way more. I didn't need it for myself. But I had Sid to worry about. A lot of money would help me find a cure, one way or another. For her and for others.

Because, though I hated to admit it, I worried there was no match for her. Or, if there were, we wouldn't find it in time. Worst, horrible case, if I couldn't find one, with the Dead Duke's money, I could give her everything this world had to offer. Make sure she got to do everything she wanted to do before her disease became a death sentence.

I wasn't convinced Riggins' deal was best for Sid and me.

He squeezed my hand again. "Haley, I need you to understand. If I have my way, there will be *no* money. None for us to split. The dukedom and all its assets will belong to the British people. I want to give it away. I'm sorry. I know it sounds selfish."

His words faded away. He was still talking, but I wasn't listening. I paled. *No money.* I couldn't be hearing him right. "But what about Sid?"

"I promise to help her find a cure. Your sister would have her health. And you would have your freedom. Your self-respect remains intact. Aren't those priceless?"

I waffled. "If we *don't* marry, by your own admission, he ruins you."

"Not if I can help it."

I paused. "Do I have a choice?"

"You can always fight me. I hope you won't. But that's an option." He looked genuinely contrite. "I'm trying to be honest with you. I'm going to fight to get out of this. I might not succeed. But I might. I won't do anything that will damage my company. If it comes down to it and I fail, we'll have to marry.

"In the meantime, all I'm asking is that you keep this from Thorne and back me up if I need it."

"And in return, if you succeed, you'll help Sid. If you don't, the agreement we have with the Dead Duke stands and we get married. If I don't help you, and you succeed, I walk away with nothing. Do I have that right?"

He nodded. "I'm not a douche. I'd rather have you for an ally. I can't do this without you." His voice was tender. "Haley? Please? Help me?"

I didn't see that I had a choice. If I didn't help him, Sid could lose. I nodded. "All right. What do you want me to do?"

His face lit up. He gave my hand a playful shake. "Play along and buy time for me to find a way to get us out of this."

If this were a regular first-date coffee date, what would this say about him? Trying to get out of relationship before it has even begun would generally be considered a deal breaker by almost any girl.

"Haley," Riggins said. "I'm really not a douche. If I find a way to thwart the Dead Duke and get out from beneath his control, I'll make sure you're comfortable. I won't leave you hanging. How does twenty million sound for your trouble?"

I gulped. It wasn't a hundred and fifty million. But then I didn't have to do as much work for it, either. It was plenty of money to me.

He looked at me expectantly. "All you have to do at that point is refuse to marry me."

I nodded. I should have been happy. All I really wanted was a cure for Sid. Or did I want more? Did I want Riggins? Or was it the fairytale being snatched from me so quickly that I was mourning?

"If I refuse to marry you, does that get you out of the contract?" I said.

He nodded. "Yes."

"You only have a few weeks," I said.

We both suddenly realized he was still holding my hand. He let go. I withdrew it and put it in my lap, heart racing.

"If you don't find a way before the deadline, then what?" I said.

"We get married. And I keep looking."

"Will you ever give up?" I was genuinely curious, though I wasn't sure I wanted the answer.

He looked me directly in the eye. "Depends. There's a point of no return, isn't there?" He laughed, finding humor in even that. "Let's hope it doesn't come to an heir."

CHAPTER SEVEN

Riggins

Haley blinked and sucked in a breath. She sat up straighter. Her back didn't touch the back of her chair. The soft light left her eyes. Suddenly, she was all business. "We have to keep up the charade so Thorne doesn't get suspicious. Should we book a wedding venue as a backup and to throw Thorne off? We'll be lucky to find anything on such short notice—"

"Not a problem. We can always get married at my place." I sat back in my chair.

She arched a brow.

"Don't look so skeptical." I laughed. "I'm serious. I can host several hundred people."

"Well...if you're planning such a *small* wedding, I guess it will do." She winked.

I let out a breath I hadn't been aware I was holding. She was a good sport. She was taking this well.

"We still need to be seen out together."

I nodded. "Absolutely. What are you doing Friday night?"

She looked startled. "Are you asking me out?"

Damn, I almost wanted to for real. I grinned and shrugged. "Why not? We can enjoy the deception and plot together evilly."

The corners of her mouth turned up ever so slightly. "Evilly?"

"Is there another way to plot?" I rubbed my hands together.

She smiled fully. Damn, I liked seeing her smile.

"I'll plan something special," I said. "Intimate. No movies. No concerts. Dinner?"

"Let me see. I don't have to work Saturday. I haven't made any other plans for Friday night. I guess I'm open." She shrugged, teasing me. "Dinner."

"Good," I said, warming to the idea. "Eating is traditional for a genuine first date. If we want this whirlwind courtship to look real, we need to conduct it like a real one."

She nodded. "Exactly. Now that the meet-and-greet coffee date is out of the way, and we've been allied in a cause, a real fight for freedom, ours, we need an activity where we can get to know each other in more depth. Talk to each other. Something beyond 'let's find a way to get out of this marriage.'" Her mismatched eyes twinkled as she held my gaze.

They were multicolored, like her hair. Not startlingly different. It was only when you really looked at her that you saw the difference.

"Nothing too over-the-top romantic," she said while I was distracted by her eyes. "No need to waste that gesture just yet. Save that something-we'll-remember-for-the-rest-of-our-lives moment for the next date. Then be as over-the-top as you like."

I laughed. "Are you telling me how to date?"

She shrugged. "I'm telling you how *I* like to be dated. So, yes, if that's what you mean. I'm not insulting your dating prowess. I have no idea how the women you've dated before have wanted to be treated." She paused. "Grab your phone. I'll give you my number."

She waited while I pulled it out of my pocket, then rattled off her number while I typed it into my phone.

"Text me now so I have yours." She grinned at me. "I know you have mine. You have no excuse if you don't call me later." She made the hand gesture for "call me."

I laughed at her antics. "You're not very trusting," I said as I texted her.

"Should I be?" Her phone buzzed. She glanced at it. "'Hey'? That's as erudite and romantic as you can be?"

"You didn't ask for either," I said. She was going to be a handful.

I walked her out. She'd taken a bus in to town. I ordered her an Uber, saw her safely into it, and drove across town. I had an old friend I had to see.

The Lipstick Spy School was in a fashionable area of downtown along Fifth Avenue, nestled among the pricey shops and boutiques. It was a highly feminine establishment—a spa, a beauty retreat, an adventure-vacation destination. It was part of a franchise that had schools in half a dozen cities nationwide.

As the name suggested, women went to it to be pampered and pretend to be spies. They learned how to dress like femme fatales. How to mix the perfect drinks. Self-defense skills. How to dance exotic dances. Not surprisingly, it was a popular destination for bachelorette parties. Or simply a day of pampering.

It was owned and operated by an old college friend of mine. Not for the first time, I needed her help. Inside was lightly perfumed and elegantly, tastefully decorated to appeal to the kind of woman who imagined herself a Bond girl. It was pure fantasy. The receptionist, a beautiful girl in a low-cut red dress, greeted me.

"I have an appointment with Milia." I smiled at her.

The receptionist nodded, picked up an old-fashioned red phone, and spoke to someone. "She's in her office on the fifth floor. Take the private elevator." She pointed. "I'll call it for you."

A few minutes later, I arrived. As I stepped out of the elevator, Milia's personal assistant greeted me and showed me into her office.

"Riggins!" Milia rose to greet me, her eyes twinkling. Her smile genuinely delighted.

As near as I could tell with Milia, anyway. She was an expert faker. She had several advanced degrees, including one in psychology. Or maybe psychology was just one of her minors. I lost track. The woman was a genius. And gorgeous, too. The entire package, especially if you liked deception.

She wore the signature red dress of the spy school. Low-cut and tight. She was model thin. Dark, straight hair in a chignon. High cheekbones. Dark eyes. Pale skin. She looked classically French.

Her assistant left, closing the door behind her.

"Emmy!" I gave Milia, which was the professional name she used now, a hug.

When I'd met her, she'd been just plain old Emily Carter. Now she was a chameleon. And, evidently, French.

"You're one of the few people I let call me that." Her voice was low, cultured, calculated to be sensual, and had just a hint of French.

Emmy was a good old American mutt. But she could pretend to be almost anything and anyone.

"What brings you to my lair, Your Grace?" There was a tease in her voice. "Or should I call you Witham?"

"Definitely not. Your Grace will do, commoner."

She laughed softly and raised one perfectly sculpted eyebrow, looking suddenly like the college girl I'd been madly in love with for a time.

"If I'd known you would someday be a duke—"

"You never would have dumped me?"

"Did I do that?" She put on an innocent look.

We both knew she'd broken my young heart.

"Being a billionaire isn't enough to tempt you?" I said. "Or fill you with regret?"

She laughed. "Maybe. It should be. If I were the type for regrets."

"And what's wrong with being Emmy? Before you decided to be French—"

She put a finger with long, French-tipped fingernails to my lips. "Ssshhh! That's just between you and me."

"All right," I said. "But call me Riggs, like always."

"Just don't call you late to dinner!" she said.

It was an old, bad joke between us from my starving college days when I'd had no money and an appetite that wouldn't quit.

She laughed again and dropped the hint of French accent. "So? What brings you here?"

"I need a favor," I said. "A couple of favors. I'm willing to pay."

"You know I love you, Riggs. But I'm a busy businesswoman these days. I only take on tasks that intrigue me." She offered me a chair and took one opposite me. "And if you pay for them, are they really favors? Or jobs?"

"Call them whatever you like. I think you'll find them interesting." I sat on the edge of my seat.

She cocked her head and gave me her full attention.

"I need you to take a girl in hand and treat her like a duchess. I'm fulfilling a fantasy of hers to be completely pampered for a day."

Emmy didn't look particularly surprised by my request. "So the rumors are true? You're looking for a duchess? Have you found one?" She became French again and pouted very prettily. She was such a tease. "I never should have let you go."

I laughed. "Is that what you call throwing me out?"

"We were young. You were an ass in those days."

"I'm not disagreeing." I had no defense. "I need your complete discretion. Nothing I say leaves this room."

"Naturally." She looked almost offended. "Who's the lucky girl?"

"Her name is Haley." I told Emmy all about her. I told her everything. About the Dead Duke and his threats. Haley's sick sister. My plan.

Emmy wasn't the kind of woman to offer optimistic platitudes or false hope. I appreciated that about her. She'd seen a lot of the underbelly of the world. It had hardened her. And she hadn't been a sucker to begin with.

Her eyes lit up at the thought of an adventure and my description of the Dead Duke. "A real-life super villain! Controlling the world from beyond the grave. I love it!"

"I knew you would." I'd called it right. "I want the press to see Haley turned into Cinderella at the ball. You're playing the part of fairy godmother. Give her the deluxe treatment at the spa—hairstyle, makeup, manicure and pedicure, massage, mud bath, the works. Bill me. When I pick her up, I want her completely gorgeous."

"No problem," Emmy said, looking bored and disappointed. She put on the pout again. "But not much fun. Were you just toying with me earlier?"

I grinned. "I knew you'd say that. This is where it gets interesting. Do you still have your connections in China and the UK?"

"What are you saying?" Her smile was absolutely sly. "Why would I?"

"Because you'd never let your spy connections die. You know how to get past the red tape in China and find out things no one else can."

I took a deep breath. "I want out of this arranged marriage. If that's going to happen, I have to find a cure for Haley's sister. Our best shot is a sibling. I need to find out whether Haley's sister has any and if any of them match her as a marrow donor. If so, I'll pay them whatever it takes to donate theirs to her.

"Additionally, I need to find a way to stop the Dead Duke from dumping his shares of stock on the market and ruining me. But first things first. If I agree to marry Haley, and she refuses to marry me, what can I do? The contract is null and void."

"And you get everything?" Emmy said with a gentle lift of her chin. "My darling, greedy Riggs!"

"Since you've become Milia, Emmy, you've become a cynic. I keep everything I currently have. All the Dead Duke's money separate from the estate goes to charity. Haley keeps her freedom. Her sister lives a long and happy life. Everybody wins."

"Do they, Riggs, darling?" Emmy cooed. "I think it would be nice if some girl tamed you and kept you for a pet."

I laughed at her. "You would."

Haley

When I got home, Sid was full of questions. "How did your meeting go? What did the duke leave you? And how did you manage to score a coffee date with Riggins Feldhem? Sunshine Sheri's twitter feed is full of the gossip."

Her voice was pitched high with excitement. She talked so fast, her sentences ran together. She was hard to understand, but her excitement was evident. Understandably. In our mundane, everyday lives, this was something exciting.

"'SeattleDuke' is still trending." She didn't slow down. "At least half a dozen people snapped pictures of you and posted them to Sheri's feed."

Those sneaky coffee drinkers! I thought.

"The buzz says you two looked *very* intimate and happy together." She raised her eyebrows in a mixture of question and innuendo.

We were better actors than I thought. Fortunately, Jasmine and Liz were still at work. I could speak freely. "That was just for show."

She frowned and made a pouty face of disappointment. "Are you sure?"

"Positive."

"I don't understand. What's for show? Why would you and Riggins be faking a relationship?"

I sighed. "It's a long story." I paused. "Can you keep a secret?"

She scoffed. "Can I keep a secret? You know I can. I'm the queen of keeping secrets."

Little secrets. Tiny secrets, maybe. But something as large and crazy as this?

"I'm serious, Sid. If I confide in you, you can't tell anyone. *Ever*." I gave her a piercing look.

"*Fine*. You know I can." She crossed her arms and put on her peeved expression. "Do you want me to promise to stick a needle in my eye?"

"Maybe."

She shook her head and raised an eyebrow. "This must be serious stuff."

I nodded. "And bizarre." I bit my lip. There was simply no good way to share this kind of crazy. "The late duke left me an arranged marriage."

Sid rolled her eyes and looked peeved. "Stop kidding around."

I put on my most serious face. "I'm not kidding. He wants me to marry Riggins Feldhem. And he's willing to pay me handsomely to do it and produce an heir." I rolled *my* eyes.

"I know! It sounds insane. I'm evidently the last female in the Dead Duke's late first wife's family line. Riggins is the last in his. He wants his biological legacy to continue the way it should have if his first wife had lived to bear an heir that survived the duke."

Sid looked at me like I'd been smoking something. I didn't blame her. The entire situation was beyond crazy.

"What?" she finally said, still looking puzzled and skeptical. "He wants you to be Riggins' duchess?"

I nodded. "And Riggins isn't thrilled with the prospect of basically an arranged marriage, as you might imagine. But for now, we're throwing the Dead Duke's executor off by playing along."

I took Sid's arm and led her to the sofa. "Sit. I'll explain everything. It's a long, complicated story."

She listened quietly while I told her everything I knew, asking only a few clarifying questions.

"Wow!" she said when I finished.

I nodded.

"That's...beyond words." She looked as stunned as I felt, and just as disbelieving as I'd been in the beginning. "What are you going to do?"

I shrugged. "Probably nothing. Riggins is trying to find a way out of it."

She didn't seem to hear what I'd said about Riggins.

"You can't do it for me." Her voice was fierce. "If you do it at all, you have to do it for yourself."

"I *will* do it for you, Sid. If I have to." I grabbed her hands. "I would give you my marrow if I could. I'd give you a kidney. A blood transfusion. Whatever it takes to make you well." I smiled, trying to reassure her.

"Having a temporary romance with Riggins Feldhem? Worst case, marrying him? You can't really compare that to losing an organ. Not unless there's something hideous about him we don't know. Most women would kill for the chance."

Sid got a devilish look in her eye. "Yeah. Some people would say you've won the lottery."

I nodded. "Exactly! This is nothing compared to what I'm willing to sacrifice for you. I would never, *never* forgive myself if something happened to you and I hadn't done everything I could to save you. Even pretending to be in love with one of Seattle's hottest bachelors." I winked.

She laughed, but her eyes misted over. "Yeah. Tough duty. The extremes you will go to." Her expression became serious. "Seriously, though, I know you'll do whatever you can. I would for you, too."

We hugged.

She pulled away and gave me an intense look. "What if Riggins fails and doesn't find a way out?"

I shrugged. "Then I marry him."

"I won't let you sacrifice your life and freedom and choices for me. I mean, marrying a guy you don't love? Even if he is hot and rich..."

I put the back of my hand to my forehead. "The sacrifices I make for you—"

She ignored my melodramatics. "Having a baby to save me? It's *your* body. I would never ask *that* of you."

"I know," I said, taking her hand again. "But I would be a surrogate for someone if that's what it took to save you. How is this different?"

She wrinkled her nose. "It's different. And you know it."

I shrugged. "It won't go that far."

She paused and got a dreamy look on her face. "But being a duchess! Can you imagine? It's almost like being a princess. Did Riggins inherit a huge estate? Did he show you a picture?"

"He inherited an estate. I don't know how large it is or what it looks like."

"How can you not know? You didn't ask? Aren't you curious?" She shook her head and clicked her tongue. "Let's Google it!"

She wriggled her hands free of mine and pulled out her phone. Half a second later, she'd pulled up a picture of a fabulous estate, the kind you would see in a BBC period piece or *Pride and Prejudice*.

We both stared at it in awe.

"I wish we could see the inside," I said.

"And of all this, you could be mistress," Sid said, sort of quoting Jane Austen.

She looked me in the eye. "Look, this is all a lot to think about." She put on her logical, pragmatic expression. "On the one hand, marrying a guy you barely know and having his baby is not acceptable to me on any level. Not if you're doing it purely for me.

"You have to think through all the implications. What if you marry him and then the right guy comes along? Will Riggins be a real douche of a husband? If so, how long would you have to stay in an unhappy marriage?

"And further, once you divorce, if you divorce, how will guys view you after your divorce? Will most guys be intimidated by your wealth? Will you have fortune hunters after you? How will you ever know that a guy really loves you? Will you have to give up your title? How will joint custody work? You'll be connected to Riggins for the rest of your lives. You won't be able to just walk away unscathed."

She took a deep breath and leaned back. "On the other hand, he *is* hot. Even for an older guy. And filthy rich. Sophisticated. Ambitious. Smart. You and he could make absolutely beautiful babies together!" She clasped her hands together and grinned at me.

I shook my head. "I would hope they look like him."

"You always sell yourself short," Sid said. "Anyway, that's my longwinded way of saying you could do a lot worse. Plus, duchess! When will you get another chance at a title? And then there's all that money. Kind of hard to walk away from that. You would be set for life. Several lifetimes. If it didn't work out, you could marry for love the second time."

"You just said I would never know if another guy was really in love with me or just my money—"

She talked over the top of me. "Or not marry ever again and just be an eccentric ex-duchess who travels the world and does what she pleases.

"What about the baby?" I asked.

"That's what nannies are for."

"I see," I said. "There's only one problem with your plan. You're ignoring the main point—he doesn't *want* to marry me. He's trying to find a way out of it."

Sid waved her hand like that wasn't a problem. "The way I see it, you have two options. Better yet, you have a double-edged plan.

"Part A—*make* him fall in love with you." She put her thin hand on my shoulder, feather light. "The odds he'll find a way out in a week are slim to none. Part B—make it impossible. Find a way to thwart his plan to get out of it.

"This is really all about you and what you want to do. *If* you want the money. *Or* you want him. *Or both. Make* him fall in love with you, Haley. You can do it."

CHAPTER EIGHT

Haley
I questioned my own motives. Were they pure? Or majorly tainted with my own greed? The adventure hadn't even begun and I was no longer sure whether I was doing this purely for Sid. Or if there was a selfish part of me in the mix. A girl who wanted to be a duchess and wear a tiara. Be married to an exceptionally handsome duke. Live in a manor house. Be mistress of all the eye could see. Not ever have to worry about money again. Was that me? Or was I only worrying that was me?

When I woke up in the middle of the cold, dark night for work on Wednesday, I almost convinced myself I'd dreamed it all up. In my desperation for someone to save us, I'd invented a duke. A reluctant duke. Now why would I do that?

I was halfway through my workday when I got a call from The Lipstick Spy School, which I knew only by reputation. It was a high-end spa and themed facility where you could learn all the necessary skills to be a femme fatale, like making the perfect cocktail and wear killer lipstick without poisoning yourself. My girlfriends and I had dreamed of having a girls' day there, but it was way out of our price range. Maybe someday. Like when I was duchess, or got my big payout. The thought of either a payout or being duchess still seemed like a dream. And I reminded myself I had to find a lawyer schooled in marital law and prenups.

A woman with a sensuous voice and a melodic laugh answered my rough hello. "Hello, Haley. Your fairy godmother calling. Riggins asked me to get you in for a day of pampering before your Friday night date. What does your schedule look like for Friday?"

My fairy godmother? He was taking things to the extreme. Hadn't I told him to keep our first real date simple, but romantic? Maybe I was just too much of an embarrassment to him. Maybe he was trying to sell this deal to the public by making me look more like his usual type? Denial was such an ugly thing.

"I get off work at two," I said, hating myself for caving without the slightest struggle. I really wanted to go to Lipstick.

"Riggins said to have you home and ready to be picked up by seven. That doesn't give us much time."

How much work did she think I needed?

"Sorry! I have to work for a living."

"Not if you catch Riggins, you won't!" Her laugh floated through the phone. "Priorities, girl, priorities. You can work in a bakery for fifteen dollars an hour the rest of your life. Or you can let me help you land a billionaire duke. Your choice."

She knew something. What had Riggins told her?

"I can be there by two thirty," I said.

Riggins

Damn it. Three precious days down. I had hoped to be out of this marry-to-save-my-business situation by now. I sat across my desk from Harry and pounded it with my fist. "*Nothing?*"

Harry shook his head. "We've searched the whole of England and the United Kingdom," he said. "You are the rightful heir, Your Grace. The expedited DNA test verified your right to the dukedom."

I glared at him.

He didn't take it personally. "You didn't seriously think your dad wasn't your biological father, did you?"

I waved my hand. "No, of course not. Mom wouldn't..."

"Thorne insisted on that damn test. He was confident of the results beforehand. I imagine he'd already snagged my DNA, one way or another. Had a PI grab a coffee cup I'd left behind and tested it. Like the cops do. He needed a legal test that I had consented to." I took a deep breath. "The entailment?"

"Our team in London says the terms of entailment are unassailable and unbreakable. As they have been for over one hundred years. You can't liquidate the estate."

I made a fist. Hoping to find some way to get rid of that albatross and use the funds from the sale to buy back Flash stock had been a long shot.

"What about the marriage contract?"

Harry shook his head. "Gray area. By the time you fought it through the legal system, the damage would be done. Thorne is as loyal as they come. I have no doubt he'll carry out the late duke's instructions to the letter. He stands to get a big payout." Harry paused. "The good news is, your prenup is almost ready and it should be ironclad."

I scowled. There was a knock on the door. Justin stuck his head in.

"You're late," I said. "I hope you have good news."

He grinned and stepped inside, closing the door behind him. "I might." He took a seat. "We contacted the orphanage Sidney was adopted from. They're sticking to their story that Sidney was abandoned on their steps, like so many girl babies born during the one-child era.

"They extend their sympathies, and thank you for the generous donation to the orphanage, but they are unable to help."

Bribery was expected in China. I had hoped it would jog someone's memory or allow someone to "accidentally" leave a file unattended just long enough for our investigators to get a look.

"They're very sorry. But they have no more information to give you.

"Our investigators are trying to track down former nurses and caregivers at the orphanage. Anyone who might have been a potential witness. It was over nineteen years ago. Memories are understandably dim. Abandoning a baby is illegal in China. Faced with punishment, why would a woman voluntarily come forward now?" Justin's voice was sympathetic.

"Look, Riggs, I hate to be the voice of realism here. There's no indication the orphanage is covering any thing up or withholding information. Your money talks. They would like more of it, obviously." He shrugged.

"There might not be anything to find out, from their end. In their experience, abandoning a baby girl wasn't a terribly unusual thing. One abandonment among many wouldn't have been particularly memorable. Even if someone thinks they remember something, they could be confusing the details."

"That's the good news?" I said. "Thanks, bud."

His grin deepened. "I'm not done. Remember that facial-recognition software I've been tinkering with the last year or so?"

"Vaguely." I didn't keep up with Justin's hobbies. He was always working on one piece of software or another.

He laughed. "You should. I've bored you with the details many times." He grabbed a can of energy drink from the mini fridge and popped it open. Justin drank so many of them, I couldn't understand how he wasn't always buzzed on caffeine. Maybe he was.

"It doesn't matter," Justin said. "Our PI obtained a record of all the employees at the orphanage from the months surrounding when Sidney was dropped off.

"We have the picture the orphanage worker who found her took when she found her. From the account in the records, Sidney was discovered swaddled in a clean baby blanket in a protected alcove, out of the weather. A spot she was sure to be found quickly. It wasn't a well-known place. Most of their abandoned wards are found on the front steps. This was around back, by the kitchen.

"I ran the blanket. It was too generic to find. A common brand that could be purchased anywhere. I kept coming back to the placement of the baby. It was unusual. It seemed like only an insider, or someone familiar with the place, would think to leave a baby there."

My heart pounded with excitement. "An insider! We can find an insider."

Harry was on the edge of his seat, too.

"It gets better." Justin set his can on my desk. His eyes shone with excitement. "I took a picture of Sidney and ran it against all the childbearing-age employees at the orphanage during that time from a staff picture the orphanage gave me, programming it to look for specific family resemblances. Several years ago, a university in Beijing had success rates as high as sixty-eight percent using a similar technique." He paused. "So there's still about a one in three chance that I'm wrong—"

"Damn it, Jus!" I almost came out of my chair. "Don't keep us in suspense."

He grinned. "I found someone who I believe is related to Sidney."

"Her mother?" I really did come out of my chair then.

"Her mother. Her aunt, maybe. It's hard to tell."

A smile spread over my face. "Where is she? I'll get my PI right on it. If I have to, I'll fly out myself to convince her to tell me what she knows."

Haley

I arrived at The Lipstick Spy School at two thirty-three. Not bad for a girl who rode the bus over. When I stepped inside the building, the space took my breath away. It smelled of delicate, seductive perfume, the kind that made you think the scent of it alone would cause any man to give up his secrets. Soft, sensual music played in the background. It was decorated in reds, pinks, black, and white. Everything was elegant.

I checked in and was given the world's softest terry robe to change into and a glass of fine French wine. My glass of wine and I were shown to a private room and told the owner of the school, Milia, would be in shortly to take personal care of my mission.

I had a mission?

I made myself at home in a reclining chair and killed the time sipping wine and flipping through the latest fashion magazines. They were so new and pristine, they still had all the special offer cards and free samples in them. Brand-new, up-to-date magazines. Now *that* was luxury.

Milia kept me waiting less than fifteen minutes. She announced her arrival with a gentle knock on the door.

"Haley?"

"That's me. Come in." I set my empty wine glass down on the stand next to me.

Milia slid in and softly closed the door behind her. She was the kind of exotic, beautiful woman that carried a ripple of sexual tension along with her wherever she went. Who could compete with a woman like her? She made me feel young, gawky, and insecure just by looking at her.

She was average height, but very thin. With pale skin and sleek, dark hair that fell in waves around her shoulders. She wore a tight red dress cut low to emphasize her cleavage. She must have been taped in place, because it looked like any sudden motion would cause her to pop out.

Looking at her was like waiting for a door to slam. There was all that anticipation. The impression, I was sure, she meant to create. She was like a siren. No straight male could look away from her. All she had to do was start singing, even badly, and they were doomed.

Her lipstick was also red, the shade only an extremely confident woman could wear. Her heels were designer and very tall, with impossibly thin, spiky heels that put her foot nearly *en pointe*.

She was a sensual creature. I wasn't sure whether to envy or fear her.

Her smile was lovely. Her eyes piercing as they took me in from head to toe. When she spoke, her voice had a trace of a French accent. "If it isn't my new godchild!" She laughed in a way that made it clear she wasn't uttering an endearment.

I was more like a burden to her. Or a pet project. I wondered how Riggins had secured this favor from her. In my next breath, I tried not to think about it. I had the feeling it had nothing to do with his money.

Milia studied me. "We have our work cut out for us."

She put on a pair of beautician's gloves and turned up the lights, which had been set low and flattering. "Let me see you better."

She took my face in her hand, ran her fingers over it lightly, and turned it from side to side as she inspected me and my complexion. I think I felt my pores actually expand under her gaze. Why weren't they contracting and running for cover?

She ran her fingers through my hair, murmuring about its texture and cut. "Who butchered this?"

I laughed. Until I realized she was serious. "I get it cut at one of those budget chain salons."

She raised one eyebrow and clicked her tongue condemningly.

I blushed.

"I suppose you use cheap drugstore products on your hair and face, too?"

I shrugged.

Finally, she pursed her mouth to one side. "Your eyes are mismatched. One green, one blue. I can fix that."

I frowned. My mismatched eyes were my best feature. According to my dad, anyway. One blue eye from him. One green eye from Mom. I was the perfect combo.

"I like that they're different colors. They make me unique." I wouldn't wear a colored contact to correct one.

"Over a half a percent of the population has heterochromia iridium. That makes it rare. But you're hardly one of a kind." Milia shook her head. "I can correct it with eye makeup. Fool the outside eye into thinking the blue one is greener and the green one is bluer."

I shrugged again, thinking I would like to see her try.

"So," she said, sitting back a bit. "Who do you want to be? A seductress? A siren? The girl next door? An exotic foreign princess? I'm a master of disguise. I can make you anyone."

I stared at her for a minute, thinking she had to be joking. Her serious expression said not.

I realized something about myself. "I just want to be me. But improved."

"Very confident in yourself, are you?" Her gaze was intense.

I shook my head. "Exactly opposite."

"Yet you think you will attract Riggins as yourself?" She leaned in close. "I'm sworn to secrecy, of course, but he told me the whole story. I know why he has to marry you. And how he's trying to find a way out of it.

"So if you think it doesn't matter how you look, the result is inevitable, think again, my darling. He claims he only wants me to sell this fairytale romance to the public. But if you want him, you're going to have to put some effort into it."

"Why would I want him? Because he's a billionaire and a duke?" I tried not to sound as irritated as I felt. But it was almost like she'd read my mind. I did want him. And maybe his money. I wanted something. "Maybe he's not to my tastes."

She laughed. "He's to your tastes. I read faces like a good cook reads recipes. You may not love him yet, but you're attracted to him. He can give you a lifestyle no one else can. You may look like a timid little thing on the outside. But I get the sense that you would like an adventure. The life of a duchess intrigues you.

"Don't sell yourself short yet," she said. "Leave your options open."

We stared at each other in silence a moment, neither of us wanting to blink first.

Finally I sighed.

She patted my arm. "That's what I thought. Trust me. I can help you. But first, we have to attack those pores."

CHAPTER NINE

Riggins
I got ready for my date on a high, thanks to my brilliant buddy Justin. He may have just handed me my ticket out of this mess.

Like any duke who was hoping to avoid an arranged marriage, I had planned this date with care. I couldn't make an enemy of Haley. I needed her cooperation. Disturbingly, I was excited about seeing her. The memory of her face and her laughter made my heart race. I liked her sense of humor and her candor. I enjoyed the thought of having an ally helping me do battle with an evil duke. And pull a prank on the public. Of playing out a fairytale.

It was late January. Which killed many of the standard outdoor first dates in my repertoire. Before anyone thinks I was a jerk, every guy who dates with regularity has a fallback list of ideas. I should have tried harder to size Haley up during our coffee date and found out what she liked to do. But I'd been busy and distracted by trying to get her to agree not to marry me.

Winter dates in a rainy city required a man to get creative. I made reservations at one of the best seafood houses in the city and asked for a table where we could be seen. I ordered flowers, ready for me to pick up on my way to Haley's. A guy can never go wrong with flowers.

Dinner and flowers might not have been inspired. But I had a surprise planned for her after.

Haley

I had never been pampered like this before in my life. Massaged until I felt like jelly. Facial. Hands dipped in wax. Manicured. Pedicured. Brows plucked. Various body parts waxed. Eyelashes extended. There was a scene in the *Wizard of Oz* books where Dorothy and company get all prettied up and, in the case of the Tin Man, oiled. I felt a lot like that. Either that or a contestant being prepped for the Hunger Games.

When it came time to have my hair cut, I resisted. Milia, who'd been absent for most of my beauty application, reappeared to give instructions to the stylist and reassure me.

She stood in front of my chair, which was spun to face away from the mirror, and bent down to get in my face. "Don't you trust me?"

I stared back at her. The truth was, I didn't. Why should I?

"I like my hair the way it is—colorful. I don't see what's wrong with it. It's a statement that life is short. Grab it. Take it. Live it. Be colorful if you like. Just don't be boring."

I'd colored my hair for Sid, after her diagnosis. During early days when things looked grim.

I stared at Milia. "You know about my sister."

It wasn't a question. I knew she knew.

"I used to have regular old dishwater hair. Very bland. I colored it to support Sid and make her laugh. It brightens her day and reminds her how important she is to me.

"I won't be turned into a boring duchess clone with traditional blond or brown hair."

Milia's expression changed only slightly, a glimmer of admiration in her eyes. "Why would I do that to you?" Milia held my gaze. "You said you wanted to be you. Only better."

She spun my chair around to face the mirror. "Look at yourself right now. No makeup. Bad hair. Tell me, honestly, that you don't *already* look like a more perfect you. Like the fantasy you."

I opened my mouth to protest. But I couldn't. She was right. I was already a more beautiful me. Not that that meant I was beautiful. But I was a step up from plain, at least. "You'll keep some color?"

She didn't concede, not outwardly. But I thought I saw something in her eyes.

"All right," I said. "But it better make Sid smile."

Two hours later, my pink and lavender hair was gone. Replaced by luxurious, shiny silver hair threaded with gold and tipped with the palest pink. I looked classic, elegant, and youthful. Artsy. Like a duchess-to-be. But from the twenty-first century, not the last century.

I'd had a makeup lesson. My eyes were heavily lined to make them look larger, fuller, and luminous. And nearly the same color. But strikingly so. My eyes seemed to change from blue to green depending on the angle you viewed me from. I wouldn't have thought it was possible to make a plain girl like me into something stunning. But Milia had done it. If I wasn't exactly gorgeous, I was, at least, intriguing. Striking. Arresting.

She reappeared to view her handiwork and smiled a slow, smug smile. "Very good." She nodded. "What do you think? Will Sidney smile?"

"Sidney will bow to your genius, clap her hands with delight, and never stop smiling. For myself, I'm almost speechless." I turned my head to look at myself from another angle. "I'll never be able to repeat it. The makeup artist was a magician."

Milia smiled, almost friendly. "You will if you practice. I'll send you home with everything you need to recreate the look, including a diagram on what goes where. You decorate cakes. You can decorate yourself. Your sister can help you. She knows a makeup trick or two, I take it?" She paused. "Now to get you dressed."

She took my arm and led me to a changing room where a tight dress, shoes, coat, and gloves waited for me.

"If you need help with anything, just yell. But first"—she pulled a bottle of perfume out of the pocket of the beauty lab coat she had put on before coming to find me in the spa—"scent makes the woman. Lucky for you, I'm an expert at scents for seduction. And I know Riggins better than almost any woman does.

"Picking the right scent is a science. And an art." She squirted the air and inhaled. "I think this one will mesh nicely with your body chemistry to create a scent, and a memory, Riggins can't resist."

She grabbed my wrist and spritzed it.

"Lift your chin." She squirted my neck. "Scent creates powerful memories. It's important on a first date to give him something he'll never forget."

She laughed. "In this case, a nose-ful of memories of you. Always choose your date perfume carefully. And make sure the memory is positive. On your fiftieth wedding anniversary, you want to be able to waft a bottle of this beneath his nose and bring him right back to the moment he fell in love with you."

Riggins wasn't going to fall in love with me. That wasn't part of the deal.

Milia grabbed my wrist and blew on it to clear the alcohol. She lifted my wrist to my nose. "What do you think?"

"It smells expensive."

"It is. It's also seductive."

I shrugged. "I've never smelled better."

She laughed. "Am I a genius or what?" She dropped my wrist. "There's a bottle in your goody bag, along with a purse-sized version. In case you need to freshen up. Just go easy on it. You don't want your perfume to announce you.

"Now change. Giselle will show you to my office when you're dressed."

A few minutes later, I was dressed in the most expensive, most seductive dress I had ever worn. Giselle escorted me as promised. The dress Milia had picked out for me fit as if it had been made just for me. And was exactly the style I would have picked. If I'd had any real fashion sense.

Giselle closed the door after herself when she left, leaving Milia and me alone.

Milia studied me. She got out of her chair and came over to me to straighten the shoulders of the dress. "What do you think?"

"I think you weren't exaggerating. You really are a makeover genius."

She smiled softly and returned to her chair.

"Is this what you do at spy school?" I asked. "Make people over?"

"I give them a fantasy." She glanced at the clock. "I'm not done with yours yet. Have a seat."

I took a seat in the chair across from her desk.

"Can you dance?" she asked, seemingly out of the blue.

I shrugged. "I can move to the music when needed."

"Which means you can't." She looked at the clock again. "We don't have much time."

She clenched her fists and stretched her fingers out wide, like someone who'd been typing too long. "Don't ask me how I know. I have my ways. Riggins certainly didn't tell me his plans. But I happen to know that he's taking you for a private dance lesson after dinner." She rolled her eyes. "It's one of those romantic dates guys think up. Because all women like dancing, right?"

She laughed. "We're genetically programmed for it. Even girls who can't dance have to give a guy credit for trying. It's an icebreaker. You can both laugh about it."

I stared at her, heart pounding. I really sucked at dancing. I had been exaggerating my skills.

"Riggins is an expert dancer. He took lessons in college." Her eyes got a misty look. Like she was remembering something pleasant. "If you can't dance, he'll pretend he can't, either. He's that kind of guy. I'm sending you to Eduardo for a quick lesson so you'll be prepared. Eduardo will also be your instructor tonight on your date with Riggins. He'll be giving you a bachata lesson.

"I'm surprised Riggins picked such a sexy dance. Given he's trying to get rid of you, I would have expected something classic. A dance where he could hold you at arm's length. Ah well." She waved her hand. "I'm also going to give you very specific instructions on what you must do if you want to hook him."

"You're confident in your own abilities." I watched her warily. "And in my desire to 'hook him,' as you say."

"With good reason. I've seduced some of the world's most important men." Her eyes sparkled.

I couldn't tell if she was teasing. She had to be, right?

She slid off the lab coat and hung it on a coat stand in the corner.

I was no longer an experiment, I guessed.

"Ignore my advice at your own peril." She returned to her chair and sat straight-backed, very regal. *She should have been the one in line to be a duchess.* "I'm going to give you the complete dossier on Riggins. Everything from how to make Riggins' favorite drink in just the perfect way to getting him in bed. For this mission, he's your mark."

She leaned forward. "There are three key things you need to know about Riggins. Use them properly and he'll make you his duchess and believe it was all his idea."

I raised an eyebrow. She had more faith in me than I did.

She ignored my skeptical look. "Number one, he likes his women confident. Don't act insecure around him. Confidence is his pheromone. It turns him on."

"I—"

"Shhh!" She put a finger to her lips. "You can be insecure in here." She tapped her heart. "And here." She tapped her head. "Just never let your insecurities show. Not so hard, really. If you try. You don't have to be beautiful to attract his attention. But you do have to be confident.

"Secondly, he likes his chocolate dark with an edge of rich bitterness. With luck, someday you'll understand what this means.

"Lastly, he values loyalty above all else, even love. Prove yourself loyal, and he'll be yours forever." She got that faraway look again.

Was it regret? It almost looked that way.

"Loyalty, of course, takes time to prove. You have very little. Time, that is. Don't waste it."

She laughed again, more at herself, it seemed, than anything else. I certainly hadn't entertained her.

"There! Don't I sound very fairy godmotherly? All I need is a wand."

I paused. "Why are you helping me?"

I had to wonder. Riggins certainly hadn't paid her to help me "hook him." That ran completely contrary to his plan.

"Karma. I owe him some happiness." She inhaled deeply. Haunted by memories again? "Riggins and I go way back. I'll always have a soft spot for him. He's all alone in this world. His father abandoned him when he was a baby. His mom is dead. He has no siblings. He's the last of the Feldhem line.

"Whether he realizes it or not, he needs someone to love. And to love him unconditionally and loyally in return." She appraised me again. "I want Riggins to be happy. I think you might be that girl who could make him happy." She got an amused look on her face. "And if not..."

She shrugged gently. "There's an above-average chance you'll be stuck with each other anyway. You may as well be happy in the process. Make yourself *that* girl, Haley."

Maybe I would. Maybe I wouldn't. Maybe I couldn't. I caught my reflection in the window behind her, barely recognizing myself. "So. Do I turn into a pumpkin at midnight?"

Her melodic laugh filled the room. "You turn into a media sensation the minute you're seen again with Riggins. And then, my darling protégé, you turn into a duchess."

CHAPTER TEN

Haley
Sid couldn't believe my transformation. "Your hair! Look at your hair." She ran her fingers through it. "It's fabulous! It feels like silk and looks like...like...there are no words. You look like you stepped out of a fashion spread in a magazine." She couldn't stop staring or smiling.

I felt guilty, actually. She would have enjoyed the experience so much more than I had. And gotten so much more out of it.

Jasmine and Liz were equally stunned by my transformation. And almost openly jealous. They grilled me mercilessly for details about everything, especially Riggins.

Jas was a nurse, very practically minded. She was having the hardest time wrapping her head around my rags to beauty to catching the eye of a billionaire story. Neither she nor Liz knew the true story. I felt terrible for keeping it from them. But it was part of the bargain.

"Let me get this straight—as part of your date, the billionaire paid for you to get ready?" She stared at me with wide eyes. "It's fantastical enough that you caught a billionaire's attention by breaking a plate at his feet."

"That's not exactly correct," Sid said. In her eyes, it was plainly clear how I could capture a billionaire's attention. "She broke a plate in front of him and then saw him again at the reading of a will of a mutual long-lost rich relative. It's destiny. Fate keeps throwing them together."

"Fate!" Jas shook her head. She didn't believe in fate, only that you controlled your own.

Sid flashed me an insider's look. "They have common ground."

Riggins had insisted on picking me up at the house. I'd had to rush home from downtown. It would have been easier for me to go directly from the spa to the restaurant. But whatever. He must have had his reasons. I was glad I got a chance to show Sid my new look before anything had the chance to mess it up.

Liz sat on the sofa with her feet up, watching TV, with a bowl of popcorn and a beer in front of her. She watched us, munching on popcorn like we were the evening's entertainment. "This is better than the movies. Are any of you as nervous as I am? I've never met a billionaire before. Do you think he'll come to the door and come in? Or will he honk from the curb?"

Jas rolled her eyes. "Come on, Liz, think! He's a duke as well as a billionaire. He'll send his valet to the door."

Sid shook her head. "His driver. He'll send his driver to the door. His valet will have to stay home and lay out his pajamas."

"And practice tying his cravats." Jas laughed.

"Come on! He's just a regular guy," I said, knowing he wasn't.

The lights from a car pulling into the driveway stopped us all short. The curtains were closed so we couldn't see his car. We were all dying to see what he drove. I would find out soon enough. The TV blared as we waited for a knock or the doorbell.

When the doorbell rang, we all jumped. Jas made a move to get it.

I gave her a death glare. "I'll get it." I should have insisted on meeting him at the restaurant.

When I opened the door, Riggins took my breath away with the look he gave me. He stared at me with a depth of expression that was hard to describe. He was surprised, obviously. And intrigued? Impressed? Maybe *stunned* was the right word. In any case, no guy had ever stared at me like that before. And I liked it. I could have kissed Milia for doing such an amazing job.

His gaze traveled down me, taking in everything from the top of my new hair to the tip of my designer-shoe-clad toes.

"Did you get your money's worth?" I whispered. It just popped out. Something about looking so amazing gave me confidence.

He gave me a grin that curled my toes and made me clench everything I owned. I was sure it was only on my side, but I felt the air crackle with sexual tension. For a fraction of a second I could picture us together forever. In the next partial second, I reminded myself that he was trying hard not to have to marry me and this was all an act.

"You look amazing. Your hair is gorgeous." He took my hand and pulled me close. "Milia deserves every penny."

He was dressed in jeans and a casual sports coat. He looked deliciously hot standing on my porch, holding the most beautiful bouquet of flowers I'd ever seen. Even before he handed it over, I could tell it was expensive.

"They're beautiful." I took a deep breath of them and smiled over the bouquet at him, determined to enjoy every minute of the evening. I took his hand and pulled him into the entryway. "Come in and meet the girls while I put these in water."

In the living room, the girls were drooling and staring at him. He should have been uncomfortable, but he seemed completely at ease. He was used to being gawked at, no doubt. And being in the company of groups of women.

He caught a glimpse of Liz chewing on her popcorn. "Am I meeting the parents?" He had the most adorable grin.

I could feel the girls melting. They'd all seen him in pictures and on TV. But pictures only partially captured his charisma. In his presence, you felt the full force of it.

Jas stepped up and introduced herself before I could, putting her hand on his arm. "I'm Jasmine, one of the roommates. Everyone calls me Jas. Haley's told us so little about you." She shot a quick, teasing glance at me. "The news says you're a duke. What should we commoners call you?"

"In the States, Riggins will do." He was amused. "In the UK, you'll have to call me Your Grace, I'm afraid."

Jas' hand lingered too long on his arm. "Are you planning to adopt a delightful British accent?"

I stepped between them. "Stop teasing him, Jas." I pulled Riggins away from her. "That's Liz on the couch."

Liz waved.

I grabbed Sid, put my arm around her shoulders, and pulled her forward to meet him. "This is my sister, Sidney."

I could feel Sid sizing him up, trying to decide whether I should sacrifice myself with him for her sake. I was losing. I could tell from her expression she thought I was crazy not to snap him up immediately, even knowing he didn't want me.

Liz and Jas had no clue. He charmed them and looked at me so adoringly that even I almost believed his act. I wondered for a brief moment if Milia had taught him how to act at her spy school.

I left him with the girls for a minute while I went into the kitchen and put the flowers in a vase of water. Laughter floated back to me. He was charming them, wrapping them in his spell.

Don't get too attached to the charming duke, I wanted to tell them. *He may not be in our lives long.*

The thought made me totally conflicted. Because, of course, I wanted a cure for Sid as soon as possible. If he could find it in the next few days, that would be a miracle. It would be perfect.

Except...I would lose out on the chance to be a duchess. I had promised Riggins. I wouldn't go back on my word. I didn't think. But what Milia had told me kept running through my mind.

When I returned to the living room, the girls were taking selfies with him. Jas was openly flirting.

I resisted the urge to roll my eyes. I grabbed Riggins' hand and pulled him toward the door. "We should be going. We don't want to be late."

I got Riggins out of the house as quickly as I could. I practically had to pry him loose from the girls.

He drove a Ferrari, a beautiful, classic red one. One question answered. He opened my car door for me and handed me into my seat.

The girls were peeking through the curtains at us as we drove away.

As soon as we were out of the driveway, I let out a sigh of relief. "Gah! I'm so sorry about the girls. They've never met a billionaire before, let alone a duke. Did you feel like a specimen on display?"

He laughed. "I'm used to it."

"I shouldn't have let you come to the house."

"You couldn't have stopped me," he said, eyes on the road. "Your sister is gorgeous and charming. I wanted to meet her. She obviously loves and looks up to you."

I nodded, feeling a twinge of jealousy that he thought she was gorgeous. I would be lying if I said I'd never been envious of Sid's looks. But I'd never felt a deep, gut-burning jealousy like this before. "Yes, she is."

"So are you, Haley." He tossed the comment off too casually for me to take seriously.

It was an afterthought. Had to be.

What did I care about beauty? There were more important things than being admired for my looks. I twisted my hands in my lap. "So, you had an ulterior motive for picking me up at the house? You wanted to meet the girl whose life is at stake in our little game?" I phrased it dramatically on purpose.

He glanced at me. "The quality of her life is at stake."

"Her odds of living a full life decrease with every passing year."

"We'll help her, Haley. I promise."

He was so confident that I believed him. I'd never thought confidence was particularly sexy before. But now? Maybe it was. As long as it wasn't overconfidence. Arrogance was a turnoff.

Riggins

Our table was waiting for us when we arrived. The restaurant was on one of the piers downtown. It had a view of the dark night water sparkling beneath the lights. Of ferries crossing the sound on their regular runs. During the day, it had a view of the Olympic Mountains. At night, with the reflections in the water, it was magical.

"Does the paparazzi always follow you around?" Haley asked when we were seated.

We'd had to fight our way through them after dropping off our car at valet parking. They'd snapped their usual zillions of pictures. And shouted questions. I'd given only glib, perfunctory answers.

I shrugged. "Not always."

I didn't want to scare her off so soon. "It's all this duke shit that has them in a frenzy right now. It will settle down again soon." I hoped. "I'm used to it."

I would have preferred anonymity and the ability to go out to dinner without being mobbed and asked ridiculous questions like, "A second date? Do you have your eye on her as your duchess? What about a British girl? A woman from the aristocracy?"

Haley is standing right here, I wanted to shout at them. *She has feelings.* Their questions made me irrationally angry. I didn't want to be that guy who was a major piece of shit and punched a reporter or decked a guy with a camera. I was supposed to be above all that. *Stiff upper lip, now, man,* I told myself. *Get in touch with your British side.*

Unfortunately, my particular British side would have taken a swing at those bastards on sight. The old man, from what I heard, never put up with shit of any kind. And the Dead Duke, he was an evil genius. I was doomed. One of these days, I was going to lose it.

"I'm not sure I could ever get used to people being in my face everywhere I went." She looked innocent, almost vulnerable.

For an instant, I wanted to punch the Dead Duke for putting her in this situation. "It's an acquired taste. It comes with the territory," I said with a grin. "I'm sorry."

Now I was apologizing over something that wasn't my fault. Things were messed up. I made a comical, contrite expression. Something about her brought out my protective side.

She laughed softly and smiled at me beneath her lashes, in an expression that mimicked the late Princess Diana. Coy and flirty at the same time. Teasing. "It's not your fault. A lifetime of having to leave the house in full makeup or be vilified is terrifying. You guys are so lucky."

I laughed. "Yeah. We just have to be sure not to develop a beer gut and go out on the beach with our shirt off."

We settled in to a pleasant meal and small talk. Surprisingly, she was easy to talk to, a good listener, and witty with her replies. She murmured sympathetic comments at all the right times. Laughed at my jokes when even I wasn't sure they were funny. And wasn't afraid to disagree with me. She told funny stories about the bakery. Her love and loyalty toward her sister were obvious. I envied Sid.

I was enjoying myself so much, I lost track of time. Looking at Haley was no hardship, either. I couldn't keep my eyes off her. Milia had transformed Haley into something exotic. She still looked young, but in a less vulnerable, childlike way. Her personality sparkled now, along with her laugh. There was a new confidence about her that was damningly sexy. I cursed Milia for doing too damned good a job on her.

I couldn't get over the difference in Haley's hair. Or stop staring at her eyes, trying to figure out what Milia had done to them. They could hold me in their depths forever, especially when they lit up when she laughed. When she talked, with her hands in full motion, her eyes were expressive and arresting. It was hard to reconcile this woman with the blushing, barefaced girl in the bakery. But they both had their own allure.

"Do I have something in my eyes?"

She'd caught me.

I shook my head. "Just admiring them. Your eyes are gorgeous."

Haley looked startled by my compliment. She opened her mouth and closed it just as quickly, breaking into a slow, soft, seductive smile. The kind that made a guy wonder what she was thinking. "Thank you."

"How are they now the same color? Colored contacts?"

She laughed again, not quite nervously. "They aren't. They're the same as they've always been. It's an optical illusion, a trick of the eye shadow and shading

Milia used. Green tones on my blue eye. Blue on the green. And suddenly, I have two blue-green eyes."

"Let me see." I too her hands in mine and leaned forward across the table to look. Her hands were slender, cool, and delicate in mine. She wore cheap costume jewelry rings on each finger. Crystals, inexpensive ones. If she were my duchess, I would rectify that. No duchess of mine would wear anything cheap.

I pushed the thought away. She wasn't going to be my duchess.

She leaned into me and batted her eyes exaggeratedly.

I laughed. "You'll have to close your eyes so I can see the shadow."

As she smiled and closed her eyes, tilting her head back slightly, I caught another whiff of her perfume. It had been tantalizing me, and teasing my senses, since I'd first picked her up. If someone had picked it specifically to turn me on and give me warm memories of this evening with her, they couldn't have done a better job. Whatever perfume it was, she hadn't worn it before at the bakery or at our meeting with Thorne. I would have remembered a scent that made me think of sex.

As I stared into her closed eyes, a flash went off. Someone had snapped our picture.

"Well?" she said.

"Yes," I said. "I see it now." I saw other things, too. The gentle curve of her neck. Her soft, smooth complexion. Her delicate fingers clutched in mine.

She opened her eyes and kept smiling at me. "Someone took our picture, didn't they?"

I nodded.

"Will we end up on the nightly news? Or the Saturday evening entertainment shows? Or just a social media post?

"What will the commentators speculate about why you're staring into my *closed* eyes? Lovers typically stare deeply into open eyes, right? What was I imagining?" She lowered her voice comically. "What were we thinking?"

Yes, what?

"Did I look rapturous? Or dreamy? Like I'm falling in love and angling to be your duchess before the other girls get a chance at you?" She leaned across the table and whispered in my ear, "Am I doing a good job of creating the kind of buzz we need? Or should I amp it up?"

If she amped it up, I was going to lose the precious thread of self-control I was hanging on to. When had she become so damn seductive?

I should have let go of her hands. I didn't. "Keep it up. I think we're fooling them and stirring up just the right kind of gossip to keep other girls away and fool Thorne."

"Can I ask you something?" She cocked her head, studying me.

"Anything."

She sighed sweetly. "Sid thinks having money will ruin my chances of finding true love. That whether I end up with millions, or hundreds of millions, I'll wonder about every guy who comes my way. Is he in love with me? Or with my money?" Even her frown was pretty, almost a pout. "How do *you* handle love? Do you ever worry you'll never find someone who only loves you?"

"I don't." I let go of her hands and pulled mine back. I didn't want her getting the wrong idea. "Maybe that's why I'm still alone."

Her frown deepened. "No one's turned your heart over yet? *Someday.* What happens then? When your heart wants what it wants? And your head doubts?"

"I'll marry another billionaire." I winked.

She shook her head. "Too glib. How many single female billionaires are there to choose from, anyway? Half a dozen? It's a small circle. Wouldn't you have met her by now? What if your billionaire only wants your title? How many billionaire duchesses do you know?"

"Mr. Thorne said it's highly unusual for a woman to inherit a dukedom and become a duchess on her own. If a woman wants to be a duchess, she has to marry a duke to do it. So, there it is, something a rich female billionaire with her eye on a title can't buy."

"I'll add 'only wants me for my title' to the list." I raised an eyebrow. "Are you *trying* to make me insecure?"

She licked her lips and shrugged. Her eyes sparkled in the candlelight, searching mine. "I can't make you anything. If you feel insecure, it's all on you. I'm only pointing out how small the odds are."

"You're my bookmaker now?"

"Maybe."

I held her gaze, giving her a piercing look, the one I used on fierce business competitors. If she wilted under it, she wasn't who I hoped she was. "Is love the most important thing to you?"

She looked at me like it was a rhetorical question.

We sat in silence while I waited for her answer.

"Oh, I see. That's an actual question, not merely rhetorical." She sighed. "Yes. Of course it is. Love brings happiness." She held my gaze. "Is that the wrong answer?"

"There is no wrong answer. Only dangerous choices. Does love bring happiness?" I thought of the heartbreak she'd feel if her sister died. I could have held out the hope I'd found for her, but I held back, saving it for the end of the evening. "I'm not so sure. I could find a fair number of people who would disagree with you."

"You would know it does, I think, if you'd ever felt the real thing."

"Have *you*?" I was genuinely curious. Was I dealing with a woman whose heart had been broken before? Or a girl who was still a naïve romantic? "I'm talking about romantic love. Not friendship. Not love for your sister."

She shook her head. "No. Not yet."

She sounded incredibly sad.

Damn, I thought. *A girl who doesn't know better.* She was ripe for some douchebag to come along and hurt her. "But you want it?"

"Yes," she said slowly. "I do." She bit her lip. "But you never know if you'll be one of the lucky ones in life who finds that kind of passionate, loyal, undying love. Or if you'll limp along with heartbreak after heartbreak. Or end up a lonely cat lady."

I laughed. "Have you noticed all the heads you've been turning tonight? You won't end up alone. You'll only be a crazy cat lady if you want to be."

She smiled softly. "That doesn't mean I won't be *lonely*." She paused. "But any sacrifice is worth it to save Sid. Even forcibly getting a pile of money thrust on me."

She laughed suddenly and stroked my leg with her bare foot beneath the table, sending an unexpected surge of desire through me.

"One thing is for certain," she said. "We know exactly each other's motives for being together. That gives our 'relationship' an honesty about it that we aren't likely to find with anyone else."

She picked up her glass of wine. "To us. Cheers."

CHAPTER ELEVEN

*H*aley
 The evening had me rattled. Being near Riggins had me rattled. I'd expected to like him *less* after getting to know him better, not more. I'd thought that when he became more of a real person to me, some of the fantasy would wear off. Instead, I found myself fantasizing about him falling for me. It was dangerous territory, falling for a man who was actively trying *not* to marry me. But I couldn't help myself.

A day ago, I wouldn't have believed it, but Riggins made me feel beautiful. The way he looked at me nearly took my breath away.

Milia had been spot on with her coaching. But I was finding I didn't need it as much as I'd feared. There was something natural and easy about being in Riggins' company. And even his cynical view of relationships didn't put me off him. Maybe, beneath it all, he was just vulnerable, like we all were on one level or another.

All I knew was that dinner flew by. I didn't want the evening to end.

After we finished our coffee and dessert, he leaned forward and took my hand. "Do you like to dance?"

And here was the conundrum—tell the truth, or follow Milia's instructions?

"I like the *idea* of dancing." I smiled back at him. "But I'm not like other girls who seem to know how to move instinctively and who've nurtured that talent through years of lessons. I never had lessons. Not one. I was never in any danger of being on my high school dance squad." My voice was just a trace sad. "Mom was sick so much when I was young, and Dad just never...

"Dance lessons were too much for him." I shrugged like it didn't matter, and blinked back real tears of missing Dad.

At the same time, damn. I couldn't get Milia's voice out of my head. I heard her gentle Parisian purr coaching me on how to win Riggins' heart.

When Riggins smiled, the corners of his eyes creased slightly and the trace of a dimple appeared. It was adorable. My breath caught. He was genuinely pleased with himself. And I was...

What was I? A liar? It was true I'd never had a dance lesson before today, but...

"Good!" His face lit up. "I have the perfect surprise—something you've never done before. I've booked a private lesson with the top Latin dancer in the city."

I smiled just enough to look uncertain, but pleased. "What? Are you kidding?"

Milia had warned me to act surprised.

He shook his head. "Well?"

"What can I say?" I pressed a hand to my abdomen and forced the nervous flutters away. "Another dream come true."

The Millennium Ballroom was located on the third floor of a historic building that had been erected in 1890. Seattle burned to the ground in 1889, so there weren't many buildings much older than it.

I had never been to The Millennium Ballroom. Sid, who *had* had dance lessons, thanks to me, had been many times. Guys took her there to impress her. Sometimes she went with her friends, trolling for guys. Sid loved dancing and always found a slew of willing partners. I was certain, should I have ventured to the ballroom, I would have been your proverbial wallflower. And probably happily so.

The paparazzi seemed to be tailing us. Flashes went off in our faces as Riggins put his hand in the small of my back, sending a shiver of pleasure up my spine, and walked me into the building that housed the ballroom. He held the door open for me and we escaped into the relative sanctuary of the elevator.

"Ever heard of bachata?" His eyes danced.

"No," I lied. "Are we playing an improve your vocabulary game? If so, I'm guessing a kind of rum?"

He grinned at me, because I was clearly teasing.

Of course I knew about bachata. Thanks to Milia, I'd spent an hour with Eduardo, Seattle's premier bachata instructor, learning how to do figure eights with my hips and dance the basic eight steps. Had I known about the Latin American dance before this afternoon? Absolutely not.

Milia had warned me. "Bachata isn't for wimps or wallflowers. It takes a confident woman to pull it off. It's all flirtation and innuendo.

"This is a test," she'd said. "Don't blow it. You have to sell the hip movement. Sell the feeling of sexual heat.

"Use it to test the chemistry between you. Let him catch a whiff of your perfume. Get a feel of your soft, silky leg. Why do you think I dressed you in a skintight dress?" She leaned toward me. "To give him ideas. So he can see the goods and, more importantly, the way the goods move."

She'd watched me closely. I didn't give her the satisfaction of flinching.

"The basic, beginning steps don't require complicated or dangerous lifts. Or jumps. Or dips. It's all about the hips for the girls and the shoulders for the men.

"And sex," she'd said. "No giggling. No faltering. Look him in the eye and sell it!"

Then she'd introduced me to Eduardo, who pushed me for over an hour, until I could make figure eights with my hips to his satisfaction and do the basic steps and the booty roll and body roll without thinking. One, two, three, tap. Five, six, seven, tap. The beat was drilled into my head.

"Tonight, when you see Eduardo for your lesson, don't give away that you know him," Milia had warned. "Surprise is all in the eyes and the subtle movements of the face. Watch me. Like this."

She'd made me practice until I'd mastered the look.

When I walked into the private lesson on Riggins' arm and came face to face with Eduardo, I wasn't surprised. But I sure looked delighted when Eduardo introduced himself and began the lesson.

Riggins leaned into me and whispered in my ear, "Are you ready for this?"

"Just how good of a dancer are you?" I said. "You sound way too eager."

He grinned. "Try to keep up."

"I'm a quick learner."

"You better be. This is a fun dance." His eyes sparkled with challenge.

Good thing for me I liked a challenge. And I had the surprise upper hand—that secret lesson.

Eduardo took my hand and positioned me next to Riggins in front of the mirrored wall. "You two make a nice looking couple. Let's see if you can dance as good as you look.

"First, Haley, the basics for the lady. For you, the bachata is all in the hips. You make a figure eight. Like this." He demonstrated.

Riggins leaned against the wall, watching with an amused expression.

"Like this?" I gave it an intentionally lame first attempt.

Riggins laughed. "You call that a figure eight?"

"Let's see you do it, Your Grace. It's harder than it looks."

He stepped away from the wall. "Is that a challenge?"

I raised an eyebrow.

He moved his hips, making a pretty decent figure eight. "I don't have quite the right build for this. But this is how it's done."

"Not bad," I said.

Eduardo stepped in. "No, no, no. For the gentleman, it's all in the shoulders. The man shakes his shoulders. The lady shakes her hips." Eduardo demonstrated again.

"You mean like this?" Riggins did the shoulder-thing expertly.

"Very good!" Eduardo clapped.

"Show off," I said. But the truth was, that shoulder-thing was hot. "I'd like to see you do that again."

He laughed.

"He can do it for you while you learn the dance. First, we start with the side by side. We just dance side by side. Very simple." He positioned us next to each other facing a mirror. "One, two, three, tap, five, six, seven tap. Haley, you lift your hip on the tap. Don't forget the figure eights as you move."

Though I could make hip figure eights in my sleep now, I let Eduardo put his hands on my hips and move them through the motions, laughing with him as I did, and casting sweet glances at Riggins as he practiced the shoulder thing. I wasn't the one who was supposed to be getting hot, but somehow I was.

Riggins was not only easy to talk to and fun to laugh with, he was eye candy, as well. Looking in the mirror at the pair of us, I couldn't help thinking the world would always see us as mismatched.

"Let's put it to music." Eduardo put some on. A slower Latin song. A beginner's song. One that gave us time to think and concentrate on our moves.

We danced, side by side, casting sidelong glances and smiling at each other in the mirror. I was keeping up, doing the steps correctly, only occasionally making an intentional misstep to throw Riggins off and let him think I'd never had a lesson.

Riggins moved easily and athletically. Sensually. His smile, the light in his eyes, and the way he watched my hips gave me goose bumps all the way to my toes.

"You're catching on quickly." Riggins' gaze held mine, then fell to my hips.

"Like what you see? Watch this." I turned my back to the mirror and did the hip-shaking figure eight, giving him a good look at my butt. I glanced over my shoulder and grinned at him. "Sidney taught me that move."

"Good for Sidney." His pupils were large, his eyes dark. "I taught myself this. From the Internet." He shook his shoulders and moved to the beat.

I watched him with an intentionally openly lustful look. "Now I know why they call you Your Grace. You're very graceful."

"I am, aren't I?" He laughed. "And that was bad."

I grinned, intoxicated by his rich laughter and the way he moved.

He caught my hands in his and spun me to face him, balancing my hands just on top of his palms, but not catching them with his thumbs. He held me nearly at arm's length, free to go. But totally captivated by him, wishing he'd pull me close.

"Let's try this face to face. Try to keep up with me." He looked over his shoulder to Eduardo. "Something a little faster, maestro."

Eduardo shrugged and put on another song that was faster, sexier, edgier. Eduardo and I had rehearsed not only the dance, but the entire lesson plan. Milia had laid it out like a battle strategy. And now Riggins was going off script. I heard Milia's purr in my ear, "Let the man lead. Follow where he goes. Riggins will push you to the limits if you let him."

I tried to get back on track. The first part of the face-to-face dance was the tease. Hold him at arm's length and tantalize him. Make him want more. So much more.

"One, two, three, tap!" Eduardo called out.

"This is crap." Riggins slid me into closed position, clasped my hand so he could lead—and believe me, I would have followed him anywhere—and looked deep into my eyes. "Much better. Don't you think?"

Damn. He'd jumped directly to the touch. Hold him close and let him feel what you've got to offer.

He nuzzled my neck. "You smell nice. You smell *hot*."

Why was I the one whose mouth was going dry? Pulled close to his hard body, it was hard to concentrate on the dance. Hard to think about anything but *him*.

There was a next step in this plan. What was it?

Riggins drove backwards, swinging those broad shoulders of his and smiling into my eyes. He pulled me forward, dancing backward. Led me sideways. To the left. To the right.

Where he led, I followed. Thanks to Eduardo, who'd taught me how to read the cues. "Look at the gentleman's chest and shoulders," he'd said. "They will always tell you where he's headed. Listen to his body language. Feel the pressure he puts on your hands. Wait for him to toss them up when he's ready for a turn or a twirl."

Looking at Riggins' chest and shoulders was no hardship. He was the best built duke I'd ever known.

Riggins pushed me faster. Harder. He pulled me in. I put my hand on his shoulder. Looked into his eyes. Smiled seductively, mimicking Milia. And tried to read what he was thinking on his face, the way she'd also taught me, wishing I was as expert as she was.

What *did* I see there? Desire? Or did I only imagine it? Could I use the moves Milia had insisted I learn to create it?

He tossed me out again. I was breathing hard. Working hard to follow his lead. He danced faster. I followed. Matching him pace for pace. Misstepping more often.

He gave my hand a gentle toss, signaling a turn. I went with it, followed his move, caught his hand, and let him spin me. He pulled me close and placed his hand at the small of my back where it rested hot and large.

I was breathing hard, but shallowly. I was excited. The dance was suggestive. But we hadn't even reached the best parts yet.

He pulled my hips close to his. Our eyes met. He smiled into mine. There was that challenge again. What was he up to?

He ran his hand through my hair. Put his knee between my legs. Rolled his hips in a figure eight into mine.

My breath caught. He wasn't playing fair. He'd taken control and was teasing me.

I fought back, cupping his head. Pulling his face toward mine. Figure-eighting my hips, grinding against his. I put my arms around his waist.

He took my hips in his hands.

This hadn't been in the plan. He'd taken me so far off track there was no going back.

He dipped me back, catching me nearly off guard.

I clutched him and looked deep into his eyes. "Latin dance is an odd choice for a British duke."

"American billionaire," he corrected. "It's hot at all the local clubs."

"It's hot in here." I came up slowly, wrapping myself around him, ending with my arms around his neck, gazing into his eyes as if I was expecting a kiss.

He smiled and tossed me out to arm's length. Casting me away? Or throwing off temptation?

Eduardo had faded to the background. It was just Riggins and me dancing now.

I gasped, surprised by his sudden move. Damn if I was going to let him win this battle.

Eduardo coughed and I remembered his coaching earlier, "Land your man with the motion of your hips and your excellent booty roll."

According to Eduardo, no hetero guy was immune to a perfectly executed booty roll. Then again, he was Latino. Latinos loved their booty. Comparatively, I was a flat-butted white girl. Milia had done her best to give me the illusion of booty. It would have to do.

Eduardo had said it wasn't the amount of booty you had. It was the way you moved it. And I had laughed, hoping he was right.

Add in a super-hot body roll and love was in the air. Oh, what the heck?

I lifted my chin, took a step to the right, and rolled my booty as Riggins watched. Stuck my butt right out there, swirled it around. Took a step to my left and broke into a body roll. Rolled from the top of my head, through my shoulder and body, shook my breasts, rolled through my waist and hips. Then repeated in reverse.

Riggins took my hand and pulled me back close to him, pulling me in so he could whisper in my ear. "As I thought. Milia gave you a lesson earlier, didn't she?"

My eyes went wide. I'd blown my cover.

He laughed as the song ended.

Eduardo clapped. "Excellent! Excellent!" Eduardo grinned. "Two of the fastest learners I've had. All I did was teach you the basic step and look where you've taken it."

I glanced at Riggins and we both broke out laughing. I couldn't stop thinking how dangerously attracted I was to him. I didn't want the evening to end. I didn't want the relationship to end. I would have done just about anything to keep it going.

"Again?" Eduardo asked. "More challenging music? I have some very nice selections."

"Again!" Riggins and I said in unison.

When he took my hand again, I felt sublimely happy. Like Cinderella at the ball. But all too soon, the clock would chime midnight. And I wouldn't become a duchess. I'd just go back to being plain old Haley Hamilton. Or would I?

Damn you, Dead Duke, for messing up my life.

Outside after the lesson, Riggins clasped my hands and turned to face me. He stared deeply into my eyes until my heart fluttered wildly. "I saved the best for last."

My heart beat out of control. Was it too soon for a declaration of his undying love?

He smiled into my eyes. "We have a good lead on who Sid's biological mom is. Now it's just a matter of locating her."

My heart stopped. My eyes misted with tears of joy. I couldn't speak.

Riggins started explaining. Something about facial-recognition software and his business partner Justin. A girl who used to clean at the orphanage and gave up her baby. How that girl was, in all likelihood, Sid's mom. I was almost too happy to hear him as he pulled his phone out of his pocket and showed me an old picture of a young Chinese girl with Sid's nose and expression.

I took the phone and held it close for a better look, barely daring to believe what I was seeing. Riggins may have "only" been a duke. But he was a prince.

Tears filled my eyes. The phone trembled in my hand. The woman looked enough like Sid that I believed...I hoped...I wanted this to be Sid's salvation so much.

Riggins was smiling at my happiness. I handed his phone back to him. He put it in his pocket and gently wiped a tear away as it slid down my cheek. He cupped my face, his hand large and warm on my cheek. His thumb stroking my chin.

I leaned into him.

His lips came down on mine, hot and tender at the same time. I had been kissed many times. But never like this. Never with this much skill and passion. Never with this much electricity in the air.

Maybe it was all the booty rolling. Maybe it was the joy at hearing such good news. All I knew was that I was falling in love with him.

At that moment, I made a decision—no matter what the Dead Duke did, I would *never* marry Riggins and have his baby. How could I spend my life in love with a man who didn't love me back? The torture may have been exquisite, but was too much to even imagine.

CHAPTER TWELVE

Riggins

I shouldn't have kissed Haley. It had been a tactical mistake. I had been hot for her. What straight guy wouldn't be after smelling that perfume all evening and watching all those booty rolls? The girl could move. She was funny and fun to be with. A danger to me and my bachelor lifestyle.

Taking a woman to bed was easy. Dealing with the emotional aftermath with a girl like Haley was messy business. I'd known kissing her was the wrong move as soon as my lips came down on hers and I felt her trembling in my arms. The last thing I wanted was for her to fall in love with me.

I certainly couldn't afford to fall in love with her. Sex between us was out. It was only our first date. She would read too much into it.

The invitation to come home with me died on my lips. I took her home instead. And found myself alone in my room, wondering what the hell had happened. There was a chink in the cynical armor of my heart. I sure as hell meant to fix it. I didn't fall in love. I didn't let women get to me. She'd been vulnerable and I'd made her happy? So damn what? That wasn't the stuff of fairytales.

The only good news of the night, besides the fun we'd had together, was that after that kiss, Haley had suddenly become distant. Which suited me just fucking fine.

I needed her to reject me so we could both get on with our lives. I needed her to refuse to marry me.

I had settled into my home office to get some work done before bed, when my cell phone rang. It was my private investigator in China.

My heart raced as I took his call, eager to hear he'd found Sid's mom.

"Did you find her?" I put my feet up on my desk and leaned back in my chair.

"Bad news, Mr. Feldhem, Your Grace," my Chinese PI said in perfect English. "We found her, all right. In the cemetery. She's been dead ten years."

Shit.

"Did she leave behind any children?"

"No children. No siblings. You know China and the one-child policy. Families are small and die out quickly.

Her parents are dead. She was an only. She left no issue. Except for the child she left at the orphanage. I'm sorry, Mr. Feldhem, duke, sir."

I rolled my eyes. The Chinese were no better at addressing a duke than my fellow Americans.

Haley

Sid was waiting up for me as I floated in from my date. She spoke before I could deliver my good news. "You're home." She frowned.

"What?"

"I was hoping you'd spend the night with His Grace." She was trying to be flippant, but her forehead was creased with concern.

"On the first date? We barely know each other."

Sid was in her pajamas. Her face was free of makeup, making her look young as she held her digital tablet. "But your date went so well—"

"How do *you* know?" I laughed, but it was plainly written on my face. I was going to hold this date in my memory forever.

"It's been trending on all the social media sites." She clutched the tablet to her chest. Talk about literally playing something close to the chest. "He took you out for seafood and then to a private dance lesson at The Millennium Ballroom. Did you like it?"

"It was wonderful!" I caught myself and wiped the rapturous expression off my face an instant too late. I cleared my throat to cover. "It was nice. It was a good thing Milia gave me a dance lesson earlier. *You* would have killed it." Though I hadn't done half bad.

I frowned. "It feels kind of creepy being followed around and having our date blasted all over social media before I even get home. Is that what's upset you?"

She pursed her lips, looking pained.

"Sid?"

She sighed and handed me her tablet. "Another woman has come forward claiming she's an heir to the duchess. She says she's going to contest the will and get a share of whatever was left to you."

"Meaning Riggins?" I laughed.

Sid remained serious. "Haley, this isn't good."

"She can't get a share of Riggins'—"

"Can't she? Did the will say that you *specifically* had to marry him? Or will *any* descendent of the Dead Duchess do?"

I bit my lip. "I hadn't even considered that. Mr. Thorne told me I was the only one so the point was moot.

"Thorne and the Dead Duke were very thorough. She has to be a fake. Otherwise, she would have turned up in their search."

"She's claiming she was born out of wedlock and given up for adoption." Sid winced. "Riggins is the duke. He's the only Feldhem heir that matters to the Dead Duke. *He* has to be legitimate.

"But if what you said about the Dead Duke is true, and his motivation is to simply have an heir that's descended from both him and his late first wife, only the genetics matter on his wife's side. Not legitimacy."

Sid grabbed my arm. "She could challenge you on this, Hale. Think about it. She could get him to marry her before you do."

"Riggins doesn't want to marry *anyone*. I don't think I have anything to worry about—"

Sid handed me the tablet. "Don't you?"

I took it reluctantly and stared into the face of a drop-dead gorgeous woman with style, sophistication, and confidence jumping off the screen. It was so potent, I swore it swirled out of the tablet in a plume.

Her name was Sybil. And her profile said she was closer to Riggins' age than I was. And British upper class, raised in an aristocratic household not so very far from Witham House. *Crap.*

I looked at my sister.

Sid held my gaze. "If she's legit, you have no power over Riggins now unless he marries you. Now that he has another choice, why would he help us find a cure for me? Or give you money not to marry him?

"What if more of these contenders pop up, Hale?" She paused. "If you want him, for whatever reason, you have to marry him. *Now.* Or lose it all."

Gina Robinson is the award-winning author of the romantic comedy Switched at Marriage serial, contemporary new adult romances *Rushed*, *Crushed*, *Hushed*, *Reckless Longing*, *Reckless Secrets*, and *Reckless Together* and the Agent Ex series of humorous romantic suspense novels. She's currently working on the next Jet City Billionaire romance.

Connect with Gina Online:
My Website: http://www.ginarobinson.com/
Twitter: @ginamrobinson
Facebook: www.facebook.com/GinaRobinsonAuthor

Made in United States
North Haven, CT
22 April 2025

68229288R00104